"Have you named him yet?"

Maya shook her head. "Nope. He doesn't have a name. I figured I'd give you the honors since you helped with the delivery."

"That's sweet considering I didn't really do anything."

"You did enough and I appreciate it." Sincerity rang out in Maya's voice and it humbled Ace.

"Frisco. I'd like to name him Frisco," Ace said, trailing his thumb against the puppy's forehead. It was a solid name for a pup who had pluck and grit. He was a survivor.

"I like that name. It suits him," Maya said, reaching out and running her palm over Frisco's head.

Maya was standing so close to him he could see the tiny, almost imperceptible freckles high up on her cheekbones. Looking into her eyes always made him feel as if he could tumble headlong into their depths. As the thought crossed his mind, he handed Frisco back to Maya. Being alone with Maya always seemed to be problematic.

He'd been so confident that he could draw a line in the sand between them…but it wasn't quite working out that way.

Belle Calhoune grew up in a small town in Massachusetts. Married to her college sweetheart, she is raising two lovely daughters in Connecticut. A dog lover, she has one mini poodle and a chocolate Lab. Writing for the Love Inspired line is a dream come true. Working at home in her pajamas is one of the best perks of the job. Belle enjoys summers in Cape Cod, traveling and reading.

Books by Belle Calhoune

Love Inspired

Home to Owl Creek

Her Secret Alaskan Family
Alaskan Christmas Redemption
An Alaskan Twin Surprise
Hiding in Alaska
Their Alaskan Past

Alaskan Grooms

An Alaskan Wedding
Alaskan Reunion
A Match Made in Alaska
Reunited at Christmas
His Secret Alaskan Heiress
An Alaskan Christmas
Her Alaskan Cowboy

Reunited with the Sheriff
Forever Her Hero
Heart of a Soldier

Visit the Author Profile page at LoveInspired.com.

Their Alaskan Past

Belle Calhoune

LOVE INSPIRED
INSPIRATIONAL ROMANCE

LOVE INSPIRED®
INSPIRATIONAL ROMANCE

Recycling programs
for this product may
not exist in your area.

ISBN-13: 978-1-335-56769-7

Their Alaskan Past

Copyright © 2022 by Sandra Calhoune

For questions and comments about the quality of this book, please contact us
at CustomerService@Harlequin.com.

Love Inspired
22 Adelaide St. West, 41st Floor
Toronto, Ontario M5H 4E3, Canada
www.LoveInspired.com

Printed in U.S.A.

And when ye stand praying, forgive, if ye have ought against any: that your Father also which is in heaven may forgive you your trespasses.
—*Mark* 11:25

For my daughter Sierra. You have always been a loving caretaker of dogs. Your big heart will serve you well in life. Thanks for always being my cheerleader. I love you to the moon and back.

Acknowledgments

For my agent, Jessica Alvarez. Thank you for your continued support and enthusiasm. I'm so happy to have you in my corner.

For my editor, Emily Rodmell. Thank you for embracing my Alaskan stories and for working so hard to make the final product shine.

I'm grateful for the assistance of Lucky Dog Refuge in Stamford, Connecticut, for allowing me and my daughter to come to your fabulous shelter and pick your brains. You are doing amazing work for rescue dogs. A big thank-you to sled dog racers Kristy and Anna Berington, as well as Kat Berington, for your grace and expertise on the subject of sled dogs and racing. What you are doing is incredible!

Chapter One

Being back home in Owl Creek, Alaska, felt more painful to Ace Reynolds than a tooth extraction. Even though he had wonderful memories of his hometown, answering probing questions about his stalled career was beginning to grate on his nerves.

Walking down Main Street felt like being on display for the entire town. He'd lost count of the number of people gawking at him. His mouth ached from fake smiling. And if someone asked him one more time about the Iditarod, he wasn't going to play nice. He might just growl at them and ruin his image for good.

Ace let out a snort. For so many years he'd been arrogant about being a dog-mushing legend in Alaska. The praise and compliments he constantly received had become a natural part of his life. Now he felt empty and broken inside since everything had fallen apart.

Who was he now, without the fame and the accolades? His mother had always said a person needed something to fall back on in case everything went up in flames. Ace had never listened to her, which he regretted deeply at the moment. Dog mushing had been his entire world. He was nothing without it.

At the moment he was making his way to Best Friends Veterinary Clinic with his dog, Luna. It had been several weeks since he'd been back in Owl Creek, but he hadn't yet taken the Siberian husky in for a checkup. He'd been lying low for as long as he possibly could in order to save face. He still felt ashamed about dropping out of the Iditarod. Most nights he tossed and turned as his mind mulled over the huge decision he'd made. He still didn't know whether it had been the right one.

Making a connection with a local vet was of the utmost importance. Luna needed top-notch care. Ace felt grateful that despite having endured an amputation, pneumonia, hypothermia and a shattered pelvis, Luna had managed to pull through.

"Hey, girl. You're doing great," Ace said,

bending down to pat her on the head. Luna looked up at him with adoration shimmering in her eyes. Ace felt his chest tighten. Luna had been with him through some of the darkest days of his life. She was the very definition of a man's best friend.

Ace trusted Vance Roberts, his family's veterinarian. So did his father and grandfather. Vance had been the vet for all of his childhood pets, as well as the sled dogs his family raced. Ace trusted his wisdom and the special connection he had with animals. His mother had always said Doc Roberts could charm all of God's creatures. His kindness and love for animals radiated from within.

He tried to block out the images that suddenly flashed before his eyes of warm, russet-colored skin and twinkling brown eyes. After all this time it still hurt to think of Maya Roberts, Vance's daughter. Sometimes he ached to relive the happiest moments of his life, the ones he'd shared with her. *Shake it off,* he told himself. At thirty-one years old, he was way too mature to wallow in past hurts. Over the years he'd learned to shutter his emotions. Although it had spared him any further heartbreaks, it hadn't led to any serious relationships. For so long it had been him and his sled dogs. Until it had all crumbled.

Ace pulled Luna's wagon behind him and pushed open the door of the veterinary clinic, then stepped inside and took a moment to soak in his surroundings. The clinic had changed a lot since he'd last been here. The interior was bright and cheerful, with vivid pictures hanging on the walls. The photos set against a cream-colored background really captured the personalities and beauty of the animals.

Ace grinned at the sight of several dogs sitting with their owners. One, a black Labrador retriever, was panting heavily with his tongue hanging out of his mouth. The other— a pit bull mix—looked at him with sad eyes. He nodded in the direction of their owners and said, "Good morning." In a small town like Owl Creek it was hard to keep his head down and avoid exchanging pleasantries, even though he didn't feel very cordial.

Who could blame him? He hadn't come back to his hometown in a blaze of glory after winning the Iditarod. He'd returned with his tail between his legs after Luna's injury and having bowed out of the competition. Ace clenched his teeth. His best friend, Leo Duggan, had told him on numerous occasions that he was suffering from a severe case of wounded pride. In Ace's mind it was so much more than that. In the blink of an eye his entire way of life had been extinguished.

With Luna trailing behind him in the wagon, Ace walked over to the reception desk to check in. The woman smiling up at him had dark hair with silver threaded through it. A warm expression lit up her face. "Good morning. Ace, right?"

Ace shook her hand. "Yes. I have an appointment with Dr. Roberts for my Siberian husky, Luna."

She grinned at him. "I'm Peggy Allen, office receptionist. You and Luna are pretty famous in these parts. You've done Owl Creek proud. And Luna has been quite a lead sled dog." She made a tutting sound. "It's a shame about the Iditarod. This entire town was rooting for you."

Ace sucked in a raggedy breath. "It sure was," he said, gritting his teeth. Memories of the accident bombarded him. Suddenly, it felt as if he was back there on the nine-hundred-and-ninety-eight-mile Iditarod Trail making split-second decisions in order to win the race. Ace had known he'd been riding his sled team too hard and way too fast in an effort to outpace the musher who was in the lead. His desire to be the first one to cross the Iditarod finish line had ended in disaster when the sled sped too fast around a curve and careened down a ravine and into a thicket of trees. The crash had been devastating, not only for his injured dogs, but also for his own sense of self-worth. Armed with the knowledge that he'd been at fault, Ace hadn't hesitated to retire from dog sledding.

"You can take a seat, Ace. Doc Roberts will be right with you," the woman said with a smile. Her words dragged him back to the present.

Ace sat down in one of the chairs and tried his best to be patient. It was definitely not his strong suit. He'd been in a lot of vet offices over the years, but this situation felt more nerve-racking than usual. Luna was still recovering from the bad accident. The fact that he blamed himself for the crash only served to heighten the situation.

He idly picked up a glossy canine magazine with a gigantic Great Dane on the cover. Ace felt the corners of his mouth twitching in amusement as he flipped through the pages.

Nothing lifted his mood more than the sight of a bunch of playful dogs.

"Hey, Peggy. I'm ready for my next appointment."

The hair on the back of Ace's neck rose at the sound of the sweet, honeyed tone. He would know this particular voice anywhere. Ace looked up from his magazine as he braced himself for the sight of the woman he'd been trying to forget for the last five years.

"Ace. It's been a long time." The familiar voice washed over him like a bucket of ice-cold water.

For a moment, all he could do was stare as he locked eyes with the only woman who'd ever owned his heart. It felt as if all the air had been sucked from his lungs as he struggled to regain his equilibrium. Maya was standing in front of him wearing an official white jacket with the Best Friends logo stitched on the pocket. With her auburn hair and jet-black lashes framing chestnut-colored eyes, Maya was still the most beautiful woman he'd ever seen. Her hair was shorter than she'd always worn it, but it suited her heart-shaped face.

"Maya," he said, surprised at his ability to make a single word come out of his mouth. "I didn't expect to see you here." Despite his attempt to play it cool, his heart was thundering inside his chest. He hoped she couldn't hear it thumping away. It surprised him to realize how deeply her presence still affected him.

Ace was having a hard time wrapping his head around seeing Maya again. She was standing mere feet away from him. Why was she back in Owl Creek working at her dad's practice? Shouldn't she be in California or Seattle or wherever she'd landed after graduating from vet school?

She wrinkled her nose. "Really? I guess you didn't hear that I moved back to town to run the practice. My dad's retiring, and he only works a few hours a week now."

Ace felt his eyes threatening to bulge out of his head. A heated sensation flared on his neck. Why hadn't he known this piece of information? "No. I had no idea," he answered. "Actually, I've only recently returned myself." Ace immediately wondered why his father hadn't told him about Maya's return. Blue Reynolds had known that Ace had an appointment here this morning, and he couldn't think of a single reason why his dad had kept quiet. Ace would have benefited from a heads-up.

"I know. I was really sorry to hear about the crash," she said, a sympathetic expression passing over her face. "Why don't you follow me and I can take a look at Luna." Ace nodded, then followed behind her as she walked down the corridor and into an exam room. Once he'd stepped inside, Maya shut the door, then bent down and patted Luna on the head.

"Hey there, girl. Do you remember me? It's been a while, but we used to be good friends, weren't we?" Maya asked as she nuzzled her nose against Luna's. Ace watched in astonishment as Luna enthusiastically licked Maya's face. She wasn't usually a demonstrative dog, but she was showing Maya a massive amount of love.

"I think she remembers you," Ace said, feeling dumbfounded. It had been almost five years since Luna, Ace and Maya had all been together. Ace shouldn't be surprised. Even as a puppy, Luna had always been crazy about Maya.

"Aww, aren't you a special girl," Maya cooed. She stood up and moved toward the scale, coaxing the dog to her side. Luna made a tentative step toward Maya before Ace scooped her up, then placed her on the scale.

Maya looked at him. "I know you're probably feeling protective of her, but you need to let her try to move on her own. It will strengthen her ability to walk."

Ace didn't respond. Her comment made him feel slightly defensive. He'd worked tirelessly to save Luna's life and care for her over the last few months. Of course he was protective of her. He hadn't just gotten into sled-dog racing for the money or the fame. Ace genuinely adored dogs, and he couldn't imagine his life without them in it.

Maya stepped back and looked at the digital scale reading. "She's a solid sixty pounds."

"That sounds about right," Ace said. "After the accident she lost a bunch of weight. Little by little I built her back up again by adding more protein to her diet."

"Well, it sure worked," Maya said, a smile playing around her lips.

Maya gently prodded Luna to walk over to the exam table. They both watched as she made her way over. "Her gait is pretty solid. It's a good thing it was one of her hind legs. The amputation site is looking good. It's healed up nicely."

Relief spread through him. Luna's well-being was of the utmost importance to him.

"You've done a good job rehabbing her.

She won't ever be the same, but I think she's doing nicely considering how badly she was hurt." She sent him a pointed look. "As you know, some racing injuries can be deadly."

Of course I know. Ace bit back the desire to snap at Maya. He inhaled a deep breath. He had no business lashing out at her. It had been a rough few months, and the strain of his situation was beginning to affect him.

"I now know more about those types of injuries than I ever wanted to," Ace admitted. "She's been a brave girl learning to walk on three legs." He swallowed past the lump in his throat. It had been an awe-inspiring experience watching Luna learn to walk again. She still struggled a bit when she was tired, but she'd made major strides in the past few weeks.

"Well, she's clearly come a long way. And she's doing well. She sure has grit."

"That's an understatement," Ace said. "I've never had a dog quite like her."

"We're actually finished here, but I'd like to talk to you about something," Maya said. She was shifting from one foot to the other. The expression stamped on her face radiated uncertainty. "I was going to reach out to you before I saw your name pop up on my appointment calendar." Maya looked right at him, their gazes locking.

A warning bell clanged in his head. Ace frowned. "What about?" he asked. After all this time, he couldn't imagine anything Maya might have to discuss with him other than his dog's health. They had been out of each other's lives for years.

"Dad told me you were back in Owl Creek. He said you've given up sled-dog racing." She made a face. "I'm sorry you had to drop out of the Iditarod. I know how much it's always meant to you." For a moment the words sizzled between them. His career had been a major factor in the dissolution of their relationship.

Being the object of Maya's pity caused a swell of emotion to rise up inside of him. It was the last thing in the world he wanted from her. Having the woman who'd dumped him feel pity for him felt like a kick in the gut.

He shrugged. "It was for the best considering the circumstances." He knit his eyebrows together. "Surely that's not what you wanted to talk to me about."

She shook her head as strands of glossy hair swirled about her shoulders. "No, it isn't." Maya exhaled a deep breath. He couldn't help but think she was fortifying herself. "I need someone to help me with a dog-rescue program I want to launch. I've been searching for someone who has experience with canines, but I haven't been successful. It's tough finding someone qualified and available in a small town like Owl Creek. I want to start out small and hopefully grow over time." She blurted out the words so fast he wasn't sure he'd heard her correctly. "It's a paying gig, Ace. Someone like yourself would be perfect. I don't know anyone who loves dogs more than you."

He felt his jaw drop. Perfect? There wasn't a single thing about him that radiated perfection these days. The very idea that Maya was so mistaken about him caused irritation to flow through him. It just proved that whatever bond they'd once shared had been irrevocably severed. She really didn't know him at all. And perhaps he hadn't known her, either. The thought caused a lump to form in his throat.

He bent down to clip on Luna's leash. All the while he carefully avoided eye contact with Maya. "I'm sorry. I truly am. I can't spearhead any dog rescues." The words shot out of his mouth like a rocket. "I've got my hands full with Luna and my other dogs."

He looked up at her. Disappointment flared in her eyes. "Please, Ace. Don't be so quick to say no. If I can't find someone to head the project, it's all going to fall apart. If I can't shelter the dogs, they face a very uncertain future."

The thought of the program not getting off the ground tugged at him, but he shoved down his feelings, unwilling to allow emotion to creep in. He'd spent years erecting this wall around himself, and he wasn't about to tear it down. Especially not for the woman who'd broken his heart. He needed to get as far away from Maya as he possibly could. He could feel himself waffling. He couldn't deny there was a part of him that yearned to help out even though he knew it wouldn't be wise.

"Maya, I'm sorry if things aren't going to work out for the program, but I have a lot on my plate these days."

A puff of air escaped from her lips. "I heard you weren't going to race anymore. If that's true, this could be a new revenue stream for you since you're not working."

He clenched his jaw. Once again it seemed as if the Owl Creek gossip mill was working overtime. It wasn't anyone's business if he had a job or not, but clearly folks were talking. "I guess I should have taken out a full-page ad in the *Owl Creek Gazette* to announce my lack of employment." He cringed at the bitterness he heard in his own voice.

Maya's eyes went wide. "Don't make this personal. It's not about me or you. Innocent dogs are going to suffer. They need our protection."

He leaned over and scooped Luna up in his arms, then placed her back in the wagon. "As you said, we're finished here. I'm sorry, but I need to get Luna home. Thanks for checking her out. I really appreciate your expertise."

As he exited the examination room and strode down the hall, he heard Maya calling out to him. Instead of turning around, he pushed open the front door and beat a fast path away from Best Friends Veterinary Clinic. A brisk wind swept across his face as he walked toward his truck. Ace didn't even want to admit to himself how badly he wanted to turn around and agree to help her. Getting some distance between them felt crucial right now.

He was having a hard time processing the events of the last half hour. Without warning, Maya was in his life again. And now that he'd come face-to-face with her, Ace had no idea how he was going to stop himself from thinking about their tangled past and what she'd once meant to him.

Maya Roberts let out the deep breath she'd been holding ever since Ace Reynolds had appeared in the waiting room of her vet practice. Back when they had been a couple, she'd been convinced they would be together for the rest of their lives. Now he seemed jaded and cold. His love and affection for Luna had shimmered and pulsed in the room, cutting through his gruff demeanor. But he seemed like he had a chip on his shoulder the size of a mountain.

Clearly he'd been shocked by her proposition. The truth was she was desperate to bring someone on board who had extensive knowledge of dogs and could help rehabilitate them. All of her previous efforts to hire someone had been unsuccessful. She should have known better than to expect Ace to say yes to anything she proposed. What had she been thinking? It wasn't as if they'd parted on good terms. Ace had been furious and heartbroken when she'd abruptly ended things five years ago. They hadn't spoken to each other since. Until today.

Maya sank down onto a wooden stool in the exam room. Sheer frustration was draining all the energy out of her. It was agonizing to know that time was slipping through her fingers. Once again she'd come up empty. Her dream of partnering with the Great Alaskan Dog Rescue Project was evaporating.

Tears misted in her eyes as she thought about all the dogs who were facing an uncertain future after being abandoned by their owners due to an unusually brutal Alaskan winter. Some of them had even been terribly abused. Her own two rescue dogs—Betty and Veronica—had been shot and left for dead in a wooded area in Kodiak. A veterinarian in Anchorage had saved their lives and rehabbed them prior to Maya adopting the pups. It had changed her life to see them reclaim their lives.

For the last few months she'd been pitching in to give rescue dogs hope, but with her father's retirement, Maya had her hands full with clients. A foundation had offered Best Friends a grant to pay for getting the project up and running. It would be devastating to have to forfeit the money.

As it was, she was hoping to bring on another veterinarian to work at the practice. She was scheduled to interview a promising candidate next week. If her health suffered and she had a relapse, she would need someone to take over the reins. It was always lurking in the back of her mind. Although her doctor had tried to reassure her that she no longer had leukemia, Maya hadn't been able to shake her fears of a health setback. Although she knew much of her anxiety was tied up in her sister's death from injuries she'd sustained in a car accident, she couldn't manage to separate her own situation from Bess's passing. Having experienced such a tremendous loss at a young age, Maya knew it was still ingrained in her psyche. She knew all too well that youth didn't protect a person from bad things happening to them. Focusing on her dog-rescue project served as a huge distraction from her fears.

Maybe she shouldn't have asked Ace to help out with her project, but with his dog expertise, he was the obvious choice. Plus, he wasn't working at the moment, and this was a paying gig. Didn't he understand how important this was? If he truly cared about dogs the way he'd always professed, he should have jumped at the opportunity to help out. His reaction had been disappointing and frustrating.

Was it their past relationship that was influencing his decision? It was true that she and Ace shared a tangled romantic history, which complicated things. Maya winced as memories of their painful breakup crashed over her. Harsh words had been exchanged between them that could never be taken back. Although they had been in love, once Maya received her leukemia diagnosis she'd ended things with Ace. Maya hadn't wanted to put him through her medical ordeal, particularly since he'd recently lost his beloved mother to cancer.

Ace's face flashed before her eyes. After all this time he was still the most dashingly handsome man she'd ever seen, with his dark hair, tawny-colored skin and chiseled features. Ace was the type of man who turned heads when he walked into a room. He was one of the main reasons why Maya hadn't built a solid relationship in the last five years. Sure, she'd been on a few dates, but due to her health concerns Maya had always kept things casual. She couldn't imagine that any relationship would come close to what she'd experienced with Ace. For Maya, it was hard to believe in love when she'd let it slip through her fingers out of fear.

A knock sounded on the door and Maya drew herself out of her thoughts. Seconds later, the door opened and she gasped. The woman standing in the entryway was her best friend, Florence Duggan. With her caramel-colored hair and bright green eyes, Florence was lovely. Her sunny nature radiated from within. "Florence, I'm so sorry. I totally lost track of time," Maya said. She glanced at the clock hanging on the wall. She was supposed to have met Florence ten minutes ago out front so they could walk over to the Snowy Owl Diner for lunch. Her appointment with Ace had thrown her off course.

Florence's tinkling laughter filled the room. "I know how much you love your job, Maya. If you can't fit in lunch today, maybe we can reschedule it for later this week. I have to bring the twins into town for an appointment on Friday so I can swing by then." Florence was the mother of the most adorable one-year-old twins, Jace and Caden. She was raising them by herself and doing a fantastic job at it, in Maya's opinion.

"Actually, I don't have another appointment

for over an hour, so why don't we head over to the diner?" Maya suggested. "I need a break. It's been a bit hectic this morning to say the least." She rubbed her hands together. "I've been hankering for a salmon burger and rosemary fries."

After Maya grabbed her purse and a light jacket, she and Florence left the clinic and headed down Main Street walking arm and arm. One of the best parts about returning to Owl Creek had been reuniting with her best friend. Florence was the only person Maya had told about her health crisis that had cropped up five years ago. Her year-long leukemia battle had been grueling. Through it all, Florence had been supportive and loving. She'd been Maya's cornerstone. She would never forget her many kindnesses.

As they walked through the doors of the Snowy Owl Diner, the aroma of grilled food rose to her nostrils. She couldn't remember a single time when the restaurant hadn't delivered an amazing meal, whether it was blueberry flapjacks, fish chowder or a classic burger and fries. Piper North, the newly married owner of the establishment, made a beeline in their direction. A smile lit up her sweet face.

"Nice to see you, ladies. Sit wherever you like," Piper said, gesturing to the dining area. With her dark curly hair and warm brown skin, she was an attractive woman with an infectious personality. She was Owl Creek's resident sweetheart.

"Let's grab that booth in the back," Florence suggested. "That way we won't have any interruptions." Maya nodded and followed behind Florence, who led the way to the empty table.

Having the townsfolk approach her and pepper her with questions about their pets was a commonplace occurrence. More times than not it happened at the diner and any other businesses she frequented in town. Although Maya loved connecting with her clients, it also felt nice not to talk shop during her lunch break.

As soon as they sat down, Maya let out a deep sigh. Her shoulders sagged as she allowed herself to relax against the leather banquette. Sometimes it felt as if she was carrying the weight of the world.

Florence leaned across the table. "Rough day?"

"Sort of. You won't believe who I met with this morning," Maya said. She was bursting to tell someone about seeing Ace again. Florence knew all about her romantic past, so she would understand Maya's feelings about coming face-to-face with him after all this time.

Florence raised an eyebrow. "Who was it? Please don't tell me a celebrity was in our little town and I missed it." Her friend's cheeks were flushed with excitement.

Maya shook her head. "Sorry to break it to you, but it wasn't George Clooney. I guess you could say he's pretty famous here in Owl Creek, though. It was Ace."

Florence's jaw dropped. "Whoa. That must have been awkward."

"It was a bit tense," she admitted. "But the focus was on his lead dog, Luna, and her injuries from the Iditarod accident." Maya bit her lip. "I think I made a mistake by asking him to head up the dog-rescue project."

Florence let out a shocked sound. "Maya. He's your ex. You didn't!"

"I did, but he turned me down," she said, letting out a sigh. "The window of opportunity is closing, Florence. And I need help. I've been putting out feelers for weeks and I haven't even gotten a nibble. Ace is perfectly suited to being in charge of the program. If I don't find someone fast, it's all going to fall apart."

Her friend made a tutting sound. "I think it was a stretch to imagine he'd agree to it. It's not as if the two of you ended on good terms. And Ace can be pretty gruff even under the best of circumstances."

Was it that outrageous of an idea? Maya had been through a lot in the last few years, and she was willing to put aside personal feelings for the greater good. They were older and wiser now. Although she'd loved him once, those feelings had faded away over the years. Surely they could join forces for a common cause?

Maya shrugged. "Honestly, I hoped he would agree to step in."

"I'm sorry he turned you down. I wish there was something I could do," Florence said. "But I'm not qualified to help out with rescue dogs. Perhaps the foundation will give you an extension to use the grant."

She shook her head. Once again a feeling of panic was beginning to seize her by the throat. "I can't imagine they would. The need to provide shelter to these dogs is urgent. I really don't want to put this project on the back burner. If life has taught me anything it's that tomorrow isn't promised."

Florence reached out and gripped her hand. "Maya. You're not sick any longer. It makes me worry when you talk that way. You're going to live a long and healthy life. You'll get the opportunity to create this program, even if it doesn't happen right now."

Maya wanted to get up and hug Florence for being so positive and comforting. Sadly, her encouragement never seemed to allay Maya's fears completely. She'd dealt with anxiety and panic attacks ever since she was twelve years old. The leukemia had only made it worse.

No matter how many times the doctors had tried to convince her over the last several years that she was in the clear, Maya still couldn't reassure herself that she wasn't on borrowed time. Getting the dog-rescue project up and running felt more pressing with every passing day. She cared so deeply about finding permanent homes for these abandoned dogs. Maya wanted to seize this opportunity while she was still able to do so.

She felt a burst of anger toward Ace. The sled crash had been awful, but it was hard to believe it had altered him so drastically. The man she'd been in love with hadn't been self-ish and shortsighted. He had always gone the extra mile to care for canines. What had happened to Ace over their time apart to turn him into someone she barely recognized?

Chapter Two

Ace hadn't been able to stop thinking about Maya's offer during the ride back home. He'd still been trying to wrap his head around Maya taking over her father's practice when she'd thrown him the curveball about a dog-rescue program. Although he had tried not to let it show, it had been an intriguing proposition. Thankfully, he'd had enough sense to turn her down.

There was no way he could head up a dog-rescue project even though it was something he was passionate about. It would be too much for him to handle, especially since he was grieving the loss of the racing career he'd been working toward for most of his life. Not to mention he already had six of his own dogs to contend with.

Well, you're used to dealing with fourteen

on a sled-dog team. The thought ran through his mind, reminding him that he was fully capable of handling a large number of dogs. After the accident, he'd loaned out eight of his sled dogs to other mushers so the canines could continue doing what they did best—sled racing. He wouldn't feel complete until all of his dogs were back home with him. The more dogs, the merrier! Perhaps he could take on Maya's project, he thought. Ace shook off the wild notion. There was no way he wanted to partner with his ex-girlfriend. He'd always cared deeply about dogs, but his affection for canines had caused him nothing but pain and broken dreams. He had made a vow to himself to step away from working with dogs, knowing how it always consumed him.

As he rounded the curve in the road and his dad's property came into sight, Ace felt a pang of nostalgia wash over him. With the mountains and woods looming in the distance, it was one of the most breathtaking views in Owl Creek. Growing up with this landscape as his playground had been a tremendous blessing. As a result, he'd come to love the great Alaskan outdoors.

As soon as he parked, Ace stepped down from the truck and gently lowered Luna to the ground. He watched as she ambled over to the fenced-in area where his other dogs roamed freely. Maya was right. He needed to give his girl more independence and stop treating her as if she would shatter. The research he'd done on three-legged dogs—tripods—had shown him how resilient they were. So far, Luna had demonstrated pluck and grit.

Blue Reynolds wasn't hard to spot in his bright red jacket surrounded by a sea of dogs. The sight made him smile despite the chaotic emotions swirling around inside him. His father's salt-and-pepper hair, paired with a long beard, always caused Ace to do a double take. He looked so much like Ace's grandfather Travis, who'd been the first dog musher in their family. Granddad lived down the road with Ace's grandmother Pearl. A few times a week, much to his grandfather's chagrin, Ace went over to check on them and bring groceries or a cup of coffee from the diner. Both insisted on living independently despite a few health challenges.

"How did the appointment go?" his dad asked as he made his way over to the fence opening, where Ace was standing. Blue opened the gate and patted Luna on the head as she walked into the enclosure. Within seconds she'd joined the other dogs—Chai, Silky, Denali, Yukon and Rocky. Despite the trauma of her leg amputation and recovery, Luna still loved to run and play. And none of the other dogs seemed to realize Luna had a disability. They simply accepted her as she was. If only humans could be as forgiving.

Ace folded his arms across his chest and locked gazes with Blue. He shook his head and made a face. "Just peachy," he drawled.

"What's wrong with you? Did someone put salt in your coffee? You look madder than my meanest rooster."

"Why didn't you tell me Maya was running the vet clinic?" Ace asked, not bothering with niceties.

An almost imperceptible smile twitched at Blue's lips. "Oh. Didn't I mention it? Sorry, kiddo. It must have slipped my mind."

Ace let out a frustrated sound. "I don't buy it. Your mind is like a steel trap. You never forget a face or a birthday or a name. What gives?"

Blue sighed. "You needed to bring Luna in to get her checked out. I know you had a great team of vets in Anchorage after the accident, but it's important to establish a connection with a vet practice here in town. I knew if I told you that Maya was running the place, you'd back out of the appointment. Don't even bother telling me I'm wrong, Ace. I know you."

Silence stretched between them, and Ace couldn't think of a single thing to say to dispute his father's words. Seeing Maya after all this time had felt like the moment he'd stuck his finger in a socket when he was five. He'd been completely thrown off-kilter. Ace wished he could say he'd felt indifferent when coming face-to-face with Maya, but it would be a huge lie. Seeing Maya again had been like being swept up by a rushing river. It was fitting, considering he'd always been a bit over his head during their relationship.

"So other than feeling blindsided, how did it go?" Blue asked.

"Luna is doing really well. Maya gave her a great report."

Blue raised an eyebrow. "And?"

Ace leaned against the fence and avoided his father's gaze. "And what? We were cordial. She even offered me a job."

Blue's eyes bulged. "A job? Did you accept?"

"Of course not," he scoffed. "There's too much water under that particular bridge. It wouldn't work out. The job involves leading a dog-rescue-and-rehabilitation program." Even as he said the words aloud, he felt a pang of regret. A few of his sled dogs had been rescues that he'd trained. He had a soft spot for dogs that had been shortchanged by their owners. One of his best dogs, Chai, had scars on his body from repeated abuse. His hands fisted at his sides at the inhumanity of it. Above all, dogs only asked to love and be loved.

When he looked up, his dad was studying him as if he was a puzzle he was trying to figure out.

"You always tell me the past is the past," Blue said. "If she's not part of your present, where's the harm in getting a paycheck and working to help animals? It sounds like a perfect gig for you."

Ace couldn't put into words the exact reasons why he knew it would be a terrible idea to work on a project with his ex-girlfriend. How could he tell his father about all of the many ways she'd trampled over his heart and left him completely gutted? He had his pride, after all. He hadn't confided in a single soul about the devastation he'd felt after Maya broke up with him. Ace had played it cool, never allowing anyone to see his pain. He had no intention of dredging up all the turbulent emotions he'd spent so many years burying. After all this time, he still didn't know why she'd ended things.

The sudden sound of tires crunching on the graveled driveway caused both of them to swing their heads in the direction of an approaching vehicle.

"Is that Dane?" Ace asked, squinting against the harsh glare of the sun. Dane Adams was the owner of the only bank in town, Adams Savings and Loan. Once he stepped out of his car and began advancing toward them, there was no question about his identity. He was wearing his signature bow tie and horn-rimmed glasses.

"What is he doing coming all the way out here?" Ace asked. He couldn't remember ever seeing Dane outside of the bank. He took his job very seriously and tended to shy away from town events. Ace didn't think he was good friends with his dad, so it was peculiar for him to stop by unannounced.

His father's skin appeared ashen. He opened his mouth, but no words emerged. His jaw began to tremble. Blue couldn't have appeared more ill at ease if he tried.

A funny feeling began to prick at Ace's insides. Something was up. And it wasn't anything good.

"Hey, Blue. Ace." Dane greeted them with a terse nod of his head.

"Wh-what brings you out here, Dane?" Ace asked. For some reason Blue seemed to have lost the ability to speak. In all of his life he'd never seen his father so rattled.

Dane fidgeted with his tie. "Blue, I'd like a few minutes to speak to you. I came out here as a courtesy so we could discuss the foreclosure on your property in person." He darted a nervous glance in Ace's direction.

"Foreclosure! What are you talking about?" Ace demanded.

His father held up his hands. "Son, let me handle this. I need to talk to Dane in private. It's nothing for you to worry about."

"I'm not going anywhere." Ace had ground out the words and now glared at Dane. "What's going on?"

"This property is in preforeclosure and if payment isn't made in the next two weeks, it's going to be put up for auction to the highest bidder," Dane explained. "I've reached out to you a dozen times or more, Blue, in order to resolve it before things spiral out of control. Trust me, I don't want to see you lose this property."

Feeling numb over what Dane had just revealed, Ace glanced over at his dad. Blue was looking at the ground and dragging one booted foot in the dirt. From this angle, his father appeared worn down. Why hadn't he seen it earlier? It was as if he was carrying the weight of the world on his shoulders.

A sheepish expression was etched on his dad's face. "Things just went a little haywire," he said, locking eyes with Ace.

That was an understatement, Ace thought. The situation was tantamount to a three-alarm, raging fire.

"Blue, do whatever you can to make the payment. It's beyond urgent," Dane said, his features creased with worry. "I'll leave the two of you to discuss this. It seems as if you might need to talk." With a slight wave of his hand, Dane turned around and headed back toward his car.

As Dane drove away from the property, Ace ran his hand over his face and tried to take a few deep breaths before confronting Blue. Angry thoughts ran through his head. Why hadn't his father told him about the pending foreclosure?

Ace knit his eyebrows together. "Dad, what happened? How did the property end up in preforeclosure?"

"I got behind in the payments. Things have been tight around here for the last few years." He shrugged. "Before I knew it, I was in arrears with no way of catching up to what I owed."

Ace pushed past the feeling of nausea engulfing him. "Why didn't you tell me?"

"After everything you've gone through in the past few months I couldn't put another burden on you. This is your childhood home, son. With you coming back to Owl Creek, I didn't want to let you down. I tried to push it all to the back of my mind, which is why I didn't return any of Dane's calls."

Ace let out a groan. "But that didn't solve anything. The problem has only gotten worse. And if you keep sticking your head in the sand, you're going to lose this place."

Sadness radiated from Blue's mahogany-colored eyes. Suddenly, the lines on his face appeared deeper, aging him considerably. Had Ace been so consumed with his own life that he hadn't noticed what his father was facing? "I don't have the money, Ace. It's that simple. As much as I love my home, I can't save it."

Hearing his father utter those words served as a painful blow. Nothing would ever be the same again for Blue if ownership of his property slipped through his fingers.

"How much do you owe?" Ace asked, his voice sounding raspy.

Blue mumbled a figure that caused Ace to gasp. Shock roared through him. How on earth had this happened?

"I'm going to pay it off," Ace announced. "That's what's going to happen."

His father let out a low moan. "No. I can't ask you to pay my debts."

"You're not asking. I'm telling you what's going to happen. Losing this place would break you." There was a tremor in his voice as he spoke. "I can't bear to let that happen."

"I'm so sorry, Ace," Blue said, reaching out and enveloping him in a tight bear hug. "It's not right that I've put you in this position."

"You've given me everything I've ever asked for without thinking twice," Ace said, raw emotion causing his eyes to mist over. "Now it's my turn to return the favor."

"You're the best son a man could ever ask for," Blue said, his chin quivering as he turned his face away from his son. Ace knew his father didn't want him to see the tears streaming down his cheeks. He reached out and gripped his shoulder before pivoting in the direction of his dogs.

Ace opened the gate and stepped inside the enclosure as the dogs came running in his direction. He stood back and surveyed the vast area as he tossed a ball for them to chase. He couldn't let all of this land slip through his family's fingers. He would call his bank shortly and make plans to get a cashier's check for the balance needed to stop the foreclosure. It was virtually his entire life savings, all of the money he'd earned from his dog-mushing career. He'd envisioned buying a house in Owl Creek, one that he could fix up and call his own. If he was given the choice one hundred times or more, he would always choose helping his father rather than having a healthy bank balance. He looked around him at the house and surrounding acreage. For the foreseeable future, this would be his home. Over the next few years he would need to build his savings account back up again so he would have a nest egg.

But, at the moment, he was going to have to eat a little crow and tell Maya he'd changed his mind about the job offer she'd extended to him. Since he would no longer have any money in his bank account to draw from, Ace needed to be employed. He needed a paycheck. He let out a groan of frustration. He wished there were more options for him, but he'd crafted a life for himself that hadn't included anything other than dog mushing.

At least he loved dogs, he thought. That was the only saving grace in having to seek out Maya with his tail between his legs.

"Do you need me to stick around and help you lock up the place?" Peggy asked as she stuck her head inside the entryway to Maya's office.

"It's sweet of you to offer, but I'm going to check on a few of the animals before I head home. Say hello to Jim for me." Peggy and her husband, Jim, were newlyweds who'd married again later in life after both lost their spouses.

Peggy grinned. "I sure will. Have a nice night, Maya. See you in the morning."

Maya reached into the mini fridge next to her desk and pulled out a cold Coke. She always saved a soda for the end of the day as a special treat. It was her way of celebrating another day as a veterinarian. After all of her hard work and so many years of dreaming about it, she'd made it a reality. God had been good to her. Ever since she was seven years old, Maya had known she was meant to have a career dealing with animals. Having her father serve as a mentor had been invaluable to her understanding of the veterinary field. Bess, her older sister, had always told her that it was her destiny. Maya smiled at the memory of her loyal and vivacious sister. Thinking of her was a bittersweet experience. Losing Bess just after her sister's eighteenth birthday still gnawed at her heartstrings. Although she tried not to give in to her worst fears, Bess's death always served as a reminder of her own fragility. Tomorrow wasn't promised to anyone.

Maya rose from her chair and stifled a yawn. She was going to do a check on the animal guests and make sure they were all set for the evening. All the dogs had been fed, given water and taken outside within the last hour. She felt a huge grin lighting up her face as she made contact with a variety of pets—cats, dogs, birds, rabbits, a lizard and a turtle.

She'd adopted two dogs herself—Betty and Veronica—both of whom hung out at the office all day until it was time to head home. A golden retriever and a cocker spaniel, they were laid-back, friendly dogs. An especially hard winter, combined with the passing of a few elderly residents, had added to the need for dog adoptions in Owl Creek. As it was, several families in town were fostering dogs until she was able to launch the formal program, which would provide all the essentials for their care and rehabilitation, as well as working toward placing them in permanent homes.

Although it had been her pleasure to give the dogs a home, she wasn't confident about being their owner long-term. What if her leukemia came back? Wouldn't it be cruel to make them think that they had a forever home, only to pull the rug out from underneath them? Until she could find them a solid owner, Maya was their caretaker and she was loving every minute of it. If only she wasn't failing so miserably in getting the dog-rescue project off the ground. If only she had more viable candidates to lead the program. Owl Creek was a small town with limited resources and a tiny population.

Her encounter with Ace flashed through her mind. He'd always been obstinate, although Maya had always been able to get him to bend. Clearly, those days were gone. Their breakup had been so bad he'd never wanted to remain friends. Maya was convinced Ace had erased their entire relationship from his mind in an attempt to pretend as if they'd never been each other's entire world. As much as it hurt to think about it, Maya knew the good times far outweighed the bad. Ace had been the love of her life. That couldn't be wiped away simply because things hadn't worked out between them. Breaking things off with him had made sense at the time, although she often wondered if she'd done the right thing. She'd wanted to spare him the pain of having to deal with her illness, and had broken her own heart in the process.

The sound of the front door opening, then quickly closing, drew Maya's attention to the waiting-room area. She'd forgotten to put up the Closed sign and lock the door. She let out a groan. She could never turn away a customer in need and this evening would be no exception. Maya's father had set a very high standard of care, and she fully intended to live up to the legacy he'd passed down to her.

"Hold on. I'll be right with you," she called out as she walked down the hall toward the reception area with her dogs trailing behind her. It was eerily quiet, with only the sound of her shoes and the dogs' nails clicking on the wooden floor. As she rounded the corner, a tall figure came into view. At first Maya only took in an athletic build and a warm brown complexion. The man was facing away from her, but as he turned in her direction, she gasped.

For the second time today Maya felt a slight jolt at the sight of Ace standing a few feet away from her. He was wearing the same clothes as earlier today but he'd put on a dark coat. Being so close to him caused a fluttering sensation in her stomach. He was still the most impressive man she'd ever laid eyes on.

"Ace! What brings you back here? Did you forget something?" Maya asked. She couldn't imagine why Ace would have come back here hours after he'd unceremoniously left her office.

He moved closer, swallowing up the distance between them. Ace being in such close proximity to her without anyone else nearby was an assault to the senses. A woodsy smell filled her nostrils, and she inhaled deeply. Ace had always been so rugged and masculine. Nothing had changed in that regard.

Even though she had fallen out of love with him a long time ago, she still felt an attraction. And who could blame her?

A thick tension hung in the air between them. She was waiting for him to answer her question, but Ace seemed to be taking his time. What in the world was going on with him? He looked a bit shaken, as if something had rattled him. Considering Ace was one of the most unflappable people she had ever known, it was slightly concerning.

Maya knitted her eyebrows together. "Is something wrong with Luna?"

"No, she's fine. I changed my mind," he blurted out. "I want to accept the job you offered me earlier. If you still want me, I'd be happy to run the dog-rescue project."

Chapter Three

Ace might have chuckled at the shocked expression stamped on Maya's face if he hadn't been so annoyed by the fact that he was standing before her in such a humbled manner. Ace had made a point in his life not to be beholden to anyone. He was a man who made his own rules and lived by them. Some viewed it as arrogance, but Ace thought it was pragmatic. That way, a person wouldn't get blindsided or hurt. But now, through no fault of his own, he had to get his father out of this jam. He blew out a deep breath and stood to his full height of six feet.

"You what?" Maya asked. Her eyes were wide. She was eyeing him with a measure of skepticism. "But you turned me down this morning. You seemed pretty emphatic about it."

Ugh. She wasn't going to make this easy for him. The look of concern and the creases on her forehead worried him. Earlier she'd sounded desperate to find someone. Now she was questioning his interest as if she hadn't been the one to offer it up in the first place.

"I changed my mind. Did you already find someone else to take the position?" His heart sank at the prospect. He needed to bring in income fast. His mind began to whirl at the possibility that this wasn't going to work out. He'd need to find something else immediately and he honestly didn't know where to start.

"No, I still need someone. I just really want to make sure you're serious about it. I can't afford to bring somebody on board who isn't fully invested." There was an edge to her voice he'd rarely heard before. Her gaze had never wavered from him. Ace felt a grudging respect for this more confident version of Maya. When they were together she'd always been overly accommodating. Maybe veterinary school had sharpened her soft edges.

"I need the job, Maya. You know how I feel about dogs. I'm more experienced than anyone else in town, unless you have the budget to hire someone from outside Owl Creek.

And something tells me that isn't the case or we wouldn't be having this conversation."

Something flickered in Maya's eyes that hinted at annoyance. "I have no doubt about your abilities, Ace. No one understands dogs the way you do." She let out a brittle laugh. "Not even the best veterinarians."

"So the job's mine?" he asked, wanting to nail it down. He wasn't sure where all of her uncertainty was coming from. He'd always been a reliable person.

"I just need to know that you'll be committed to this endeavor," Maya said. "There's a lot riding on it."

"I'm not the one who ran away from commitment." Ace spit out the words before his brain could tell him not to go there. He wasn't even sure why he'd said it, but he knew immediately what a mistake he'd made in doing so. Immediately, Maya's face crumpled. Her mouth opened and she made a hissing sound like steam escaping a kettle.

Her lips trembled as she spoke. "What was I thinking? I should have known this could never work. You can show yourself out, Ace." She turned her back on him and began to walk away back down the corridor.

"Wait!" he called out. "I'm sorry. That was

a stupid thing for me to say. It's been a frustrating afternoon, which is not much of an excuse, but it's the truth." He let out a ragged sigh. "I need this job, Maya. Badly."

She turned back around. "That didn't seem to be the case earlier. What's changed?"

Ace didn't want to spread his family's business all over town, but he knew Maya well enough to realize she would never divulge his personal information to anyone. She wasn't that type of person. "After I left here this morning I found out my dad's place is about to be foreclosed on. If that were to happen, he'd be devastated." Ace's voice cracked. He couldn't hide his feelings about his father. Just imagining his father enduring such a loss made his heart ache. Years ago, when they'd lost Ace's mother to a ruthless cancer, he'd witnessed the type of devastation he never again wanted to see in his dad. Another blow might break him.

Maya gasped. "Oh, no! That's terrible. Your father loves that property. I can't imagine what he's going through. Is there any hope of saving it?" Maya's voice was filled with compassion. His dad and Maya had always enjoyed a close relationship when she and Ace were a couple. Blue had never understood why they'd parted ways, and on numerous occasions he'd expressed his desire to have Maya as his daughter-in-law. Ace had told him in no uncertain terms that Blue had a better chance at being struck by lightning in an ice storm.

"He's not going to lose the property. I'm taking care of the back payments, but it's going to drain my savings account." He swallowed past the bile rising up in his throat. It felt embarrassing to lay all of this at Maya's feet. She'd pressed him for answers and he'd told her the truth, but he didn't want a shred of pity directed his way. And he certainly didn't want Maya to think he was laying a sob story on her. Hopefully, she still knew him well enough to recognize it wasn't his way of doing things.

"I understand," Maya murmured. "You need steady income coming in."

"Yes," he said with a nod. "And I'll be sticking around Owl Creek, so it makes sense to find employment here. I'm dependable, Maya. I won't let you down."

Maya nodded. "I know you won't. I've never known you to go back on your word. I received a grant to get this program started." She shifted from one foot to another. "The problem is we don't have much time to get it up and running. There are dogs who are being sent here from kill shelters that don't have the space or a commitment to keep them long-term. If I can't pull it off, I need to give the money back."

Ace winced. "I can't believe all shelters don't have no-kill policies." He shook his head. "It never fails to amaze me. We humans still haven't caught up to the humanity dogs show us."

Maya frowned. "You're right about that. All shelters should provide safe harbor for as long as they need it. That's one of the reasons I'm so excited about this rescue project. We'll be able to save so many dogs and funnel them to loving families. We're essentially giving them a new lease on life."

Passion radiated from Maya's voice. It reminded him of the multitude of conversations they'd had over the years. "I remember how you talked about this when you decided to go to vet school. It was a big motivating factor for you."

"I tried for years to get my dad to focus on dog rescue, but with Bess's passing and being the sole proprietor of this place, it was a bit out of his reach. So I suppose that dream was planted in me." A sweet smile lit up her face. "And now it's going to come true."

Back in the day, they'd dreamed of making a life together. The future veterinarian and the dog musher. He felt a pinching sensation in his chest at the memory of all he'd lost when Maya walked away from their love story. And it had been love, hadn't it? Ace had never experienced anything like it—not before Maya or since.

"So…am I hired?" he asked, holding his breath as he waited to hear if they would be working together. It mattered to him way more than he could ever put into words. He locked gazes with her, trying to read the expression emanating from her eyes.

"I need to go over salary and hours with you, but, yes, I'd like to offer you the position. Because of the urgent need for shelter services, I'd like you to start as soon as possible."

A huge feeling of relief swept over him. Although working with Maya would present its own challenges, knowing he would have a steady paycheck in his future was gratifying. God was always looking out for him. This moment was no exception.

"I appreciate it," Ace said. "I'm looking

forward to meeting all of the dogs. I can honestly say I've never met one I didn't like."

Maya cleared her throat. "Despite what happened between us in the past, I'm confident we can work together and make this project something we can both be proud of."

Ace tried to smile, but it felt forced. He wasn't sure at all that he could work with Maya without blurring the lines between business and their romantic past. As it was, he could hardly stop himself from staring at her. She had always been a beautiful woman and time had only enhanced her good looks. The one thing he knew with a deep certainty was that he wasn't going to allow himself to fall back in love with Maya Roberts. He'd barely recovered from the heartache the last time. Working as the coordinator for rescue dogs was a means to an end for him. This time around he was going to lead with his head and not his heart.

Maya felt conflicting emotions as she stood across from her former flame. It was so strange to be in this situation with a man who'd once owned her heart. She knew instinctively that Ace was the perfect person for the position, but at what cost to her feelings?

He wasn't the sort of man a person could be neutral about, which perhaps explained why her pulse was racing.

"So, what location is going to be utilized as home base?" Ace asked. He looked around the office. "Off-site I presume?"

"You'll be situated at the property right next door. My dad bought it years ago, hoping he would be able to expand the vet clinic and bring on some more veterinarians." She wrinkled her nose. "Unfortunately, it never came to pass. So the building has been sitting there for years unused."

"Can I check it out? Since the clock is ticking we should make sure everything is in working order."

"Of course," Maya said. "I had the lights and water turned on, as well as the heat. I stepped out on a limb regarding this project because I truly believed it would all come together. And now it has." She needed to focus on the positive instead of worrying about the past. She trusted that Ace would have a great handle on the program so she could focus her efforts on the vet clinic. Most likely she wouldn't even see him a whole lot.

"Let's head over," she said. "I just need to grab my coat and the keys from my office."

As soon as she reached her office, Maya's cell phone began buzzing. She quickly recognized the phone number on the display. It was Ingrid Baxter, who was in charge of the dog-rescue foundation. Maya had been avoiding talking to her since she hadn't been able to find anyone for the lead position. Having just hired Ace, Maya felt relieved that she didn't have to duck Ingrid's calls any longer.

She picked up the call and said, "Hey, Ingrid. How are you doing? I was just talking to the person I hired to lead the dog-rescue program."

Maya listened as Ingrid greeted her and congratulated her for bringing someone on board. For the next few minutes, Maya paid attention as Ingrid discussed the project and the next steps. She felt her mouth hanging open as Ingrid dropped a bomb on her. Somehow she managed to form a sentence and not totally lose her composure.

"That sounds good. I'm sure we can handle it," she assured Ingrid.

After ending the call, Maya put on her jacket, grabbed the keys to the building next door and headed back toward the front. Ace was sitting on the edge of the reception desk, scrolling through his phone.

He swung his gaze up to look at her, his brow furrowed. "Is everything all right? You look a bit bowled over."

Maya bit her lip. "I just got a phone call from the woman who oversees the foundation in Anchorage that's spearheading the project."

"Is everything still on schedule?" he asked. Maya could see the anxiety stamped on his face. He was clearly worried about his new position.

"No, everything is fine, except she's asking if we can handle some additional dogs. The shelter in Homer has an abundance of rescues that they are hoping we can take in."

"How many dogs total are we talking about?"

Maya hesitated to answer. She didn't want to scare off Ace. The number was a bit mind-boggling. She honestly wasn't sure if she should have agreed to the larger number. "With the dogs we're expecting, then adding in this number…" Her voice trailed off.

"Maya, how many?" Ace pressed. "You said 'small' earlier. Twenty? Twenty-five?"

"A little bit more," she confessed. "Based on my last tally we're up to forty."

Ace began to sputter. "Forty dogs? As in four and zero?"

"Yes," Maya said in a low voice. She'd already felt as if she was in over her head with the project, but now she'd just buried herself, as well as Ace. What had she done by agreeing to accept more dogs? Judging by the way Ace was gaping at her, he was wondering the very same thing. Maya's lips began to tremble. For such a long time she'd tried to be strong and resilient. All of a sudden she felt completely overwhelmed. Tears pooled in her eyes and she ducked her head so Ace wouldn't see her raw emotions.

Suddenly, she felt Ace's hands lightly gripping her upper arms. "Hey there. Don't cry. There's nothing to be this upset about." She swung her head up and their eyes locked. Maya was startled by the look of compassion flaring in his eyes. "We've got this. With the two of us working together on this rescue project, we can't fail. Remember, God won't give us any more dogs than we can handle." The beginnings of a smile twitched at the sides of Ace's lips.

Despite everything, she found herself smiling back at him. Ace's words of encouragement buoyed Maya's spirits. Gratitude swelled inside her. Despite their fractured past, he was trying to lift her up. Somehow just hearing Ace express confidence in the situation made her believe it was possible. He'd always had that effect on her.

"You're right. We can pull this off," Maya said. And she meant it.

Something familiar flickered in the air between them and she watched as Ace appeared to recognize it as well. His eyes widened imperceptibly. He took a step backward and cleared his throat. "I should be heading home."

"Okay. Why don't we check out the facilities tomorrow?" Maya suggested, sensing Ace wanted to leave.

He nodded in agreement. "Thanks for hearing me out," he said with a nod. "'Night."

"Good night. I'll be in touch," Maya said, watching as he practically sprinted away from her and out of the clinic.

Maya sucked in a deep breath. Ace had completely caught her off guard with his unexpected return to her clinic and the way he'd changed his mind about running the dog-rescue program. His speedy exit had been just as surprising as his arrival. Just when things had appeared to be thawing between them, he'd retreated. And for the life of her, she couldn't figure out what had caused him to leave the clinic as if his feet were on fire.

Chapter Four

The following day, Maya was at her clinic bright and early. Just knowing she would be seeing Ace today made her nervous. She didn't know how to explain it, other than attributing it to the fact that she'd always sensed there was unfinished business between them.

Well, of course there is, a little voice buzzed in her ear. *You never told him the truth about your cancer diagnosis!* She let out a sigh. It had been much easier to stuff the truth down into a little black hole when she hadn't been living in Owl Creek. Now they would be working in close proximity to one another on a daily basis. Perhaps she'd underestimated how awkward it might be with the truth standing between them.

She simply had to focus on their professional relationship and her goal of making better lives for the rescue dogs. That's what mattered most now. It was humbling knowing God had spared her life and given her an opportunity to make this project into a reality.

The sound of the front door opening made her pulse quicken. Maya turned her head toward the entrance, wondering if Ace had shown up early. The tall, silver-haired man with warm brown skin was a welcome sight for Maya.

"Dad!" Maya said, greeting her father with heartfelt enthusiasm. It was always great to see him at the practice he'd built up with such love and care. "What are you doing here?"

"I had to come and congratulate you on your dog-rescue project coming together so nicely," he said. "I got your message last night. I'm proud of you, Bitsy, for realizing this dream." He placed his arm around her shoulder and pressed a kiss on her temple. *Bitsy.* Even though she was an adult, her father still called her by her childhood nickname. She loved hearing it roll off his lips.

"You always encouraged me to chase my dreams," Maya said, tears pricking her eyes as a swell of emotion washed over her. She'd wanted to follow in her father's huge footsteps for most of her life.

"And you sure did listen," he said with a chuckle. He narrowed his gaze as he looked at her. "I'm a bit surprised you brought on Ace to lead the program. He was really torn apart when you broke up with him. Feelings like that tend to linger."

Torn apart? Maya didn't recall it quite that way. Ace had been angry initially, but as was his customary way of handling things, he'd shut down on her and shrugged it off. "I guess I don't remember all of that since I left for vet school shortly thereafter."

Vance shook his head. "Well, it's all water under the bridge now. I always liked Ace, so it's nice to see the two of you coming together for a good cause. He's had a hard time of it lately."

Maya nodded. She felt a thick lump in her throat just thinking about Ace quitting the Iditarod and ending his prestigious career as a dog musher after the accident with his sled dogs. From what Maya had heard on several news reports, Ace had been traveling too fast around a curve on the trail, which had led to the terrible accident. Dog mushing had been Ace's most cherished dream and his love for the sled dogs had always come first, so she knew he'd been devastated by the dogs' injuries. He'd been spoon-fed on Alaskan dog sledding since the day he was born. Coming from a family lineage of dog mushers had always been a big part of his identity.

She couldn't deny the feeling of accomplishment she felt regarding getting the dog-rescue program up and running. Although she knew it wasn't going to be an idyllic work situation due to the iceberg-size chip on Ace's shoulder, it was an answer to prayer. Ace really was the most qualified person for the job, and but for their fractured romantic history, he would have been at the top of her list from the beginning.

Ace had always been protective of his family. He'd seemed so sure of himself when he had initially turned down her job offer. Yet, hours later he'd returned, eager to accept her proposal because he had to rescue Blue from foreclosure and needed income. That was the man she'd fallen in love with all those years ago—strong, kind and loving.

The memory of Ace comforting her— grasping her arm—washed over her, serving as a reminder that she wasn't immune to him. Not by a long shot.

She'd torched their relationship to the ground rather than tell him about her leukemia diagnosis. Her actions had wounded him, which had been the very thing she'd been trying to avoid. Maya had seen the depth of Ace's grief when he'd lost his mother to cancer. Wanting to spare him from going through that nightmare all over again had been the reason she'd ended things with Ace.

Had she made the right choice in sparing Ace from any additional heartbreak? Maya shook off the doubts. It was pointless to speculate about decisions she'd made in the past. Moving forward in life was all she could do. She needed to focus on managing her vet clinic and getting this program up and running. These dogs needed rehabilitation and forever homes. How was Ace going to handle forty dogs by himself? Sure, she could pitch in after hours, but the vet practice kept her busy during regular work hours. Thankfully, there was money in the budget to bring on a part-time helper for Ace.

Suddenly, an idea popped into her head. She didn't know if Ace would be on board with it, but Maya thought she might know the perfect person to bring on to assist with the program—Zach Reynolds. As a member of a dog-mushing family, Zach had experience as a dog handler for Ace that gave him a wide range of experience with canines. Ace and his younger brother hadn't always gotten along, but that had been well over five years ago. Now, they were all older and wiser.

Surely, Ace would do whatever was in the best interest of the rescue dogs who desperately needed his help.

Ace stood at the stove cooking eggs, grits and sausage for breakfast. He turned toward his dad, who was sitting behind him at the kitchen table guzzling down his morning cup of joe. "Is Zach home? I've made enough for the three of us."

"He tore out of here a little while ago. Don't ask me where he was going, because I don't know." His father shrugged.

Ace let out a grunt. Zach appeared to come and go as he pleased. If anyone asked Ace, he would tell them that his 19-year-old brother didn't have enough structure in his everyday life.

"Did you take your medicine?" Ace asked. Since coming back home, Ace had discovered that his dad needed daily medication to control his diabetes. He wasn't always on top of it, which meant Ace had to check and double-check.

"I took it as soon as I woke up," he answered, stopping just short of rolling his eyes at Ace. He knew his father hated being monitored, but Ace was determined to keep him out of the hospital.

Blue drummed his fingers on the table. "I feel guilty, son. I never wanted you to spend your hard-earned money on bailing me out." His father's eyes radiated regret, tinged with a hint of embarrassment.

"Don't bother with feeling guilty. You know me well enough to realize that I always do what I want," Ace said, turning around to face his father. He reached for his father's plate and filled it up with food, then placed it on the table before fixing his own. Ace sat down across from Blue and reached for his father's hands as they said grace.

After blessing the food, Ace dug in to his breakfast, eating way faster than normal. He needed to be at the dog-rescue location in thirty minutes, and he planned to be on time. He didn't want to give Maya any reason to regret hiring him on. He truly needed the position.

"You're going to have to watch my dogs while I'm at work," he told his father. "Luna will come with me and hang out with the rescue dogs. You up to it?"

His dad bristled. "Of course I am. What are you asking me that for? I'm as hearty as they come, and I know more about dogs than you and Maya combined."

Ace stifled a smile at the outrage in his dad's response. "I'm just warning you that my dogs can be a handful."

"Ha! I handled the most successful sled-dog team in Alaskan history. Don't get me started on feisty dogs!" Blue shot him a smug smile.

Ace held up his hands. It was hard to argue with his father on that topic. He was an Alaskan dog-mushing legend. "Okay. I get your point. I just didn't want you to be blindsided."

"Thanks for the heads-up," Blue said. "Again, I can't thank you enough for saving the old homestead, Ace." He peered at him over his cup of coffee. "How'd it go with Maya? I imagine it was a tad bit awkward." Blue wrinkled his nose and grinned.

Ace locked gazes with him. "Can we not do this? Maya and I have a business relationship. Nothing more. Nothing less. Please get any other notion out of your head."

Ace stood up, picked up his dishes and quickly rinsed them off in the sink. "I'm heading out. Call me on my cell phone if you run into any problems."

All Ace heard was a snort as he left the house with Luna trailing behind him. It made him chuckle. He figured being ornery was better than being apathetic. When Ace's mother passed away, Blue had gone through a period of depression that had been hard to shake him out of. At least now he was functioning.

Ace arrived at Best Friends with a few minutes to spare. When he pulled into the lot, he immediately spotted Maya standing by the structure next door to her clinic. He stepped out of his truck, then gave Luna a helping hand getting down. He walked toward Maya, inhaling a deep breath as he made his way to her side. *This is all business*, he reminded himself as he soaked in the sight of her. She looked so good he had to remind himself not to stare.

Her dark strands of hair were captured in a high ponytail that accentuated her striking facial features. Although their relationship had died, Ace was forced to acknowledge that he was still attracted to the woman he'd once loved like no other.

"Hey, Ace. Thanks for coming." Her face lit up at the sight of Luna. "Hey, girl," she said, reaching down to pat her on the head.

Luna greeted Maya even more warmly than she had yesterday. "You're looking good," Maya said to the dog.

She's not the only one. Unbidden, the words popped into Ace's head. He needed to focus on the dog-rescue project.

"Morning, Maya," he drawled, shifting his gaze away from her to the building. He'd caught a glimpse of the structure yesterday and was itching to get inside to check it out.

"I was just thinking about putting up a sign," Maya said as she tapped her chin and gazed at the building. "It would give the place some curb appeal."

"Do you have a name for the dog rescue yet?" Ace asked. "Something that will resonate with the community?" His gut was telling him that they didn't need bells and whistles to attract potential adoptive families to the center. Sometimes simple was better.

"No, I haven't come up with anything that sticks," Maya said, her eyebrows knitted together in a frown. "Any ideas?"

"Why don't we keep it nice and simple? How about Owl Creek Dog Rescue? It will look nice on a sign," he suggested. "Maybe use a bronze-and-hunter-green color scheme."

Maya nodded. "I like it. It's catchy and it

gets the point across. You always did think fast on your feet," she said. "I think it raised my dad's eyebrows a few times."

Ace stiffened up. He wasn't at a point where he could joke with Maya about the past. Honestly, he wasn't sure that he ever would be. He was only working here out of sheer necessity. After she'd abruptly kicked him to the curb five years ago, they hadn't even maintained a friendship. But for Blue getting in over his head regarding the mortgage, Ace wouldn't be here.

He chose not to respond to her comment. What was there to say, anyway? The days when he and Maya had been able to finish each other's sentences were long gone. All that remained was a partnership based on need. There was absolutely nothing personal about it.

"Now that we have the name settled, let's head inside," Maya suggested, her expression remaining placid. Back in the day it had irritated her to no end when he was unresponsive. It gave him a small bit of pleasure knowing he might have gotten under her skin, especially since she was embedded under his.

Ace followed behind her, but then reached out and pulled open the door for her. As they stepped inside, Maya flipped on the lights. Ace looked around, deeply curious to explore his new work environment. The first thing he noticed were the rows of large, shiny kennels. He'd visited numerous dog shelters before and they hadn't looked at all like this one. The space was open and airy. He began walking around, becoming more and more excited as each space revealed hidden gems. There was a small kitchen with a good-size fridge and stove. He imagined it would come in handy for storing dog food, medicine and cooking meals. He was an expert at making home-cooked meals for dogs who had special dietary needs.

"This is incredible," Ace gushed. "This play area is amazing. Hey, Luna," he said, calling her to his side. Once she was standing beside him, Ace led her to the area, where he threw a Frisbee for Luna to catch. He clapped enthusiastically when she jumped up and caught the toy, then brought it back to him. "That's my girl," he said, heaping praise on her as he ran his hand across her back.

"It's great isn't it?" Maya asked, watching the playful exchange between him and Luna. "The grant paid for some of this, but my dad chipped in to help me finance it. He's been a big supporter of the dog rescue."

"He's a good man," Ace said. Vance Roberts was a beloved figure in Owl Creek. He was wise and caring, with a gentle soul. Ace knew that he'd taken on clients who couldn't afford his office fees. The doors to his vet practice had always been wide open to anyone who needed his services. He had taught Ace a thing or two about dogs when he was barely eight years old.

"Well, I did some brainstorming and came up with a great assistant to help you with the dogs." She paused, then said, "Zach."

Suddenly he found himself praying there was another Zach in Owl Creek.

He sputtered. "Zach who?" Surely she wasn't talking about his brother?

Maya tilted her head and folded her arms across her chest. "Your brother, Zach."

"Oh, you've got jokes." He began to chuckle at the very idea of working alongside Zach.

"What's wrong with hiring your brother?"

Ace was shocked at the question. Was it possible Maya didn't remember all of his brother's immature antics? While they'd been dating there had always been something he'd gotten into that had risen to the level of a near catastrophe. Ace had been the one to bail him out time and again.

"Do you want a list? It might take me a while. Lately he's shown a poor work ethic and he's not all that reliable. Most importantly, he professes to love animals, but he barely lifts a finger to take care of them at my dad's place." Ace shook his head at the thought of Zach's irresponsibility. He couldn't pretend it didn't get under his skin.

"Well, Ace, you need a partner to work with you. Forty dogs are way too many for you to handle alone. I thought it might be easier to bring someone on that you already have a relationship with. And Zach has vast experience as a dog handler. But if you don't want to hire Zach, then you'll have to find someone else. I'm placing it in your hands."

"Oh, I'll find someone...just not Zach," he replied firmly. He wasn't going to agree to this ridiculous idea just to pacify Maya. She'd always had stars in her eyes about Zach, going back to the time they'd been a couple. Maya had always viewed him as Ace's sweet little brother with a caring heart.

Maya let out a huff of air. "I see you're still as ornery as ever. It wouldn't kill you to bend a little, Ace."

He chafed against her unwarranted criticism. He'd bent so much lately he was almost broken. But she didn't know any of that and she was no longer privy to the details of his personal life. Ace turned away rather than get into a war of words with her. If this partnership was going to work out they needed to get along, or at least keep things civil. Being annoyed with her this early in the game didn't bode well.

Maybe this wasn't such a good idea after all. Emotions were simmering inside him that he dared not let loose. He might just explode, and lashing out at Maya with five years' worth of emotions would be over the top.

Ace felt Maya touching his arm. Even though he was wearing a light corduroy jacket, his flesh still felt singed by the contact.

"I'm sorry, Ace. I shouldn't have said that." She sounded contrite. When he turned to face her, all of his anger dissipated. What was it about this woman that grabbed ahold of him and tugged at his heartstrings? He'd fallen out of love with her ages ago, but being near her still packed a solid punch.

"It's all right," he conceded. "You're free to have your own opinion." It still rankled him to know she'd been so quick to judge him.

He shouldn't be surprised. After all, this was the same woman who'd blindsided him with a breakup. He hadn't seen it coming at all and it still baffled him. How had he missed the signs of trouble? Ace had been ready to get down on one knee and pop the question. Thankfully, he'd dodged that humiliation.

"No, it's not okay," Maya replied. She let out a ragged breath. Her slight shoulders sagged. "Your relationship with Zach isn't my business. You and I are in a partnership, so I need to respect your boundaries. I'm sorry for pushing."

Her brown eyes locked with his own. What her gaze revealed comforted him. She was being sincere. He had the sneaking suspicion she was overwhelmed with everything on her plate, although he knew from past experience with Maya that she had a hard time admitting it.

"And I promise to respect yours as well. I'll start looking for an assistant right away." But it won't be Zach, he wanted to add. Not in a million years.

"That'll be great. Why don't you make a list of anything I might have missed and I'll circle back with you later on." She reached into her back pocket. "Here's a credit card you can use for any necessities, such as bedding, toys and dog food. Just keep track of what you're spending since our budget is still tight."

Ace reached out for the card and tucked it into his jacket pocket. "Thanks. I'm used to working on a budget for my sled dogs, so I know how to stretch a dollar."

"That's what I like to hear," she said with a nod of approval. "Well, I need to get back to the clinic. Braden's bringing in his dog, Rudy." She grinned at him. "Braden was one of the first people to step up and embrace one of my rescue dogs who needed a home. And just recently Connor took in a sweet terrier named Fiji. Now if we could only find forty generous souls like the North brothers."

Braden North was a good friend. He and Ace had grown up together in Owl Creek and, along with his brother, Connor, they'd enjoyed plenty of adventures in their Alaskan playground. It didn't surprise him at all that both brothers had taken in rescue dogs. Maya was right. If only there were more people ready and willing to adopt a rescue dog and change its life forever. The world would certainly be a better place.

"Once things are up and running with the

dog rescue, I want to reach out to other veterinarians in other parts of Alaska in order to find potential homes for the pups. At some point I also want to speak to Gabriel to see if we can put together a transportation plan to get the dogs out of Owl Creek."

Ace nodded approvingly. "It would be great to have other towns supporting our mission. When the time comes I can reach out to Gabriel if you like." Gabriel Lawson was a local pilot who owned his own aviation company. Ace felt certain they could work something out with Gabe.

"I would appreciate that," Maya said.

"Quick question—when can I expect the dogs to arrive?" He couldn't deny the excitement racing through him at the idea of being in the company of so many dogs. He missed his dog mushing days and being around a sled-dog team comprised of fourteen canines. It wasn't a profession for the faint of heart, but he'd always embraced it wholeheartedly.

"The first ones are set to arrive on Friday. They're coming from Fairbanks, Homer and Kodiak, I believe. And there are twelve of them."

Ace gulped. He felt a few beads of sweat

break out on his forehead. "This Friday? As in four days from now?"

Maya bobbed her head as a guilty expression crept across her face. "Yes. They're coming from far and wide, believe it or not. Our little Owl Creek Dog Rescue is going to be bursting at the seams with dogs." A smile stretched across her face.

Ace couldn't contain the chuckle that escaped his mouth. Maya looked over-the-moon happy about the prospect of the dog rescue having a surplus of canines. There was no denying how gorgeous she looked when she was joyful. It brought back a host of memories that he hadn't thought about in a long time.

"Well, it's a good thing I love dogs," Ace drawled as Maya turned on her heel and headed toward the door. Once he was alone Ace began walking around and taking stock of the place with a critical eye. Given the numbers, some dogs would have to double up in the larger kennels. It shouldn't be a problem, he realized. They were pretty roomy. And the play area was equipped with several items to help with rehab issues. He would need a detailed rundown from Maya before Friday about the dogs and any health issues they were facing. He ran a hand over his face.

This was going to be way more complex than he'd imagined. Maya had done an amazing job with setting it up, but there were still things he needed to get done by Friday.

First and foremost, he needed an assistant and some good-hearted volunteers. Most dog shelters had volunteers from the community who donated their time and energy due to their love for canines. Now that the harsh winter months were over, perhaps more people would be willing to pitch in a few hours a day.

Twelve dogs would soon be occupying this space and filling it up with an abundance of canine energy and playfulness. He was going to be providing a refuge for dogs in need of nurturing and attention. It wasn't hard for him to imagine how it would look and smell and feel.

"This is a good thing we're doing, Luna," Ace said, nuzzling her head with his knuckles. "Something we can be proud of. I haven't felt that way in a long while." Luna looked up at him, seeming to sense his upbeat mood. She'd been with him through some of the darkest days of his life, and he was convinced Luna could read his emotions.

For the first time since his career as a dog

musher had crashed and burned, Ace felt a glimmer of hope sparking inside him. It was odd to feel grateful to Maya after everything that had gone down between them, but being offered this position could be a turning point in his life. It would be hard work to dedicate himself to forty rescue dogs while maintaining a professional distance from Maya, but he was determined to get the job done and guard his heart at all costs.

He'd already been burned once, and he refused to go down that road with Maya ever again.

Chapter Five

Sunset was beginning to creep in, and the sky was ablaze with vivid oranges and pinks, as well as a streak of lilac. Maya peeked out of her office window and stifled a yawn. Although being a vet fed her soul, it had been a grueling day. She'd operated on one of her four-legged patients—an Irish setter named Pepper—who had a ruptured disc in her back. The pooch had done well in surgery and was now resting comfortably in the recovery room. In the morning, Pepper would go home with her owner, Beulah North, the grand dame of Owl Creek. In the meantime, Maya would stick around to check in periodically on her patient.

Her fatigue was playing tricks on her, transporting her back in time to when she'd received her leukemia diagnosis. *Stop it*, she chided herself. Just because she was tired didn't mean her leukemia had returned. Despite her best efforts, thoughts of Ace kept creeping past her defenses. A long time ago she'd put up a wall in order to safeguard her heart from regret and doubts about her decision to end things with him. But in the last two days those questions had come roaring back to life. Would she and Ace have settled down by now? Pledged themselves to one another? They'd never talked about marriage, but they had dreamed about merging their careers—veterinarian and dog musher extraordinaire. It had promised to be a wonderful life.

"What might have been" was a hard concept to tackle. In the beginning, those troublesome questions had kept her up at night, tossing and turning in the hours between darkness and dawn.

A loud sound drew her attention outside. She walked to the door and wrenched it open just in time to see Ace lugging some fluffy dog beds into the building. The sight of rugged Ace holding lush dog bedding brought a smile to her face. Sweet Luna was sitting patiently by Ace's truck.

She couldn't believe he was still here at

this hour. Honestly, she shouldn't be surprised. He'd always had an outstanding work ethic, which had catapulted him to the top of the dog-sledding world. Ace Reynolds was a household name in Alaska and in certain countries around the world. She grabbed a light jacket and headed outside. After a tough winter, the mild April weather was a nice change of pace. She walked toward the dog-rescue building, just as Ace was coming back outside.

Surprise registered on his face. "What are you still doing here? I thought your office closed a while ago."

"I needed to stick around tonight to check on a very special patient. It's Beulah's dog, Pepper. I operated on her today, and I want to make sure her vitals are good before I leave. She's doing really well so far. She has a little bit of physical therapy in her future, but she's up for the challenge." Maya felt a deep sense of professional pride knowing that she'd been able to ease a dog's suffering.

"A-a-ah. I've missed seeing Beulah, our honorary town mayor," Ace said. "Glad to hear about Pepper."

Maya slapped her hand to her forehead. "I can't believe I forgot about doggy beds for the kennels. Where did you get them?"

"I went to the Trading Post and convinced Twyla to give me a fifty-percent-off deal. They're great sponsors, by the way. You might want to consider approaching them about giving the dog rescue a donation. They've been supporting my career for a long time."

"Seriously? Fifty percent off is pretty sweet. I guess I shouldn't be shocked. She always did have a crush on you." Maya would never admit it in a million years, but it used to bother her when she had to watch Twyla Lewis shamelessly flirt with Ace. He'd always been nonchalant about it, which had riled her up even more.

Ace chuckled good-naturedly. He seemed to be loosening up around her. "What can I say? She likes tall, dark and handsome dog mushers."

Maya shook her head at him, pretending to be full of disapproval.

"Hey. I ordered a pizza. Would you like to share it with me? I can never finish a pie by myself." Maya surprised herself by throwing out the invitation. Things still felt a bit awkward between her and Ace, which would ultimately be detrimental to their partnership. Maybe sharing a meal and talking about the dog-rescue operations would smooth things out.

Ace's eyes widened and he cuffed the back of his neck. He shifted from one foot to the other. "I should probably get going to check in at the house."

"Is your dad okay?" she asked. After what Ace had confided to her about Blue nearly losing the family home, Maya had been fervently praying for him.

"He's fine. Just as stuck in his ways as ever. He's watching my dogs today."

"Then all the more reason to stay and share a meal with me. There really are so many things we need to work out," Maya said.

Just then the crunching of tires heralded the arrival of the pizza-delivery person. Maya was so hungry she started doing a little dance in celebration. Ace looked in her direction and shook his head. It was one of the major differences between them. Maya would dance with abandon in the rain while Ace wouldn't even tap his foot to the beat. Opposites attract. It's what her mother always said, and it had been true about the two of them.

Maya stepped forward to pay the delivery person and take ownership of the medium Margherita pizza with extra cheese. She'd also been given a small bag with plates, napkins and forks. When she turned back toward

Ace, Maya held up the pizza. "It smells delicious, doesn't it?"

Ace let out a groan as Maya headed toward her truck and let down the back hatch. She placed the pizza down and hopped up so that her feet were dangling. His eyes were focused on her like laser beams as she bit into her first slice of the mouthwatering pizza.

"You know I can't resist Italian food," Ace grumbled as he quickly reached the truck and hopped up beside her. She handed him a plate and he quickly added a few slices.

They sat for a few moments in companionable silence as they demolished the pizza. Maya held up a piece of crust. "Is it okay if I offer it to Luna?"

"Sure. It's past her dinnertime so I'm sure she'll appreciate it." Maya jumped down and went on her haunches so she was at eye level with the husky.

"Here you go, sweet girl. Enjoy it." Luna eagerly accepted the crust and began crunching on it, which made both Maya and Ace laugh.

For the next half hour, they talked shop about daily routines, exercise, food, rehabilitation, medicine management, making lists specific to each dog, bath time, grooming and a variety of other topics. Ace brought up crowdsourcing and they discussed various innovative ways to get financial support. Maya brought Ace up to speed on some of the special needs she'd been informed about regarding the rescues. "Of course, I'll be providing my services pro bono, which will save us a lot of money. You wouldn't believe how vet costs really affect the ability of shelters to care for their residents. Prescription costs alone are a killer."

"Oh, I know all too well," Ace said in a low voice. "After the Iditarod crash I was hit with exorbitant bills for Luna and a few of my other dogs. Luna's injuries were the most severe due to her leg injury and amputation. Thankfully I had a lot in savings due to various prize monies I won over the years."

"I can only imagine what a nightmare that must have been for you," she said. "And then to feel compelled to walk away from dog sledding as a result of the accident. It must have been brutal." She made a tutting sound. Just thinking about all he'd been through made her shudder. His entire life had been upended in an instant.

Ace visibly winced, making her believe she'd dug too far into his personal pain.

"It taught me to appreciate the moments more because we never know when they're going to fade away. I was on top of the world, riding high. Until I wasn't. And in the aftermath it was so clear to me what was important and it wasn't winning another Iditarod." He crumpled up his napkin. "I made a bargain with God that day. If He spared Luna, I wouldn't ever place glory over the safety of my dogs."

His words told her so much about the burdens he was carrying around. Ace blamed himself for the crash, probably due to the speed at which he'd been traveling leading up to the curve on the trail. Maya knew that the Iditarod was a grueling competition that culled the most exacting performances from the competitors and their sled dogs. Accidents happened. Dog mushers and their canines got hurt all the time. There were even fatalities. She could tell by looking at Ace's impenetrable expression that he'd convinced himself he was to blame. It was something he'd need to work out over time.

Hearing Ace talk about living in the moment reminded her so much of the agonizing days after Bess's death. One moment they'd been laughing and teasing at the kitchen table and a few hours later the car Bess had been a passenger in slid off an icy Alaskan road, through a guardrail and down a ravine. Her beautiful, fun-loving sister had been killed instantly. For Maya it was still hard to fathom that they'd lost Bess before she'd even gotten a chance to live.

"I'm so glad Luna made it," she said. "One of the hardest things for me to wrap my head around is when God doesn't answer my prayers in the way I want. I still struggle with it."

"That's understandable. I've felt the same way. It's hard not to feel angry when you pray and it seems like He isn't listening."

"It is," she admitted, speaking past the lump of emotion clogging her throat. "But, I know not all prayers are answered the way we hope they'll be."

"And it doesn't mean He isn't listening, even though it might feel like it." Ace finished her thoughts for her. She looked over at him, surprised by his words. It harkened back to the days when they'd shared so many intimate conversations about their faith. He sounded like the old Ace, the one who'd owned her heart. One of the main reasons she had fallen for him was because he was a man of strong faith.

"I imagine you think about Bess all the time. And how you would give the world to have her back." Compassion flared in his eyes. Ace knew firsthand how deeply she and her parents had grieved Bess's death.

"I do," Maya confirmed. "There isn't anything I wouldn't trade just to talk to her one more time." Bess had been the best listener in the world, and she'd been loyal to the bone.

"I get it," Ace said. "My mother always gave me the best advice. I always ask myself what would she have done when I'm conflicted."

"She was the real deal. So loving, as well as being one of the kindest people I've ever known," Maya said as an image of Gloriana Reynolds came into sharp focus in her mind. Tall and shapely, Gloriana had one of the best voices in town. She'd been the lead singer in the church choir and her melodic harmonies were soul-stirring.

"It's my goal in life to become half the person Gloriana Reynolds was," Ace said, his voice trembling. Ace and his mother had been very close, and his grief had been all-consuming when she'd passed away. Maya had done her best to shepherd him through his mourning, but to this day, she wasn't certain if she'd been able to help at all. Ace had a habit of going inward, and that time was no exception.

"Is it out of the question to think we could be friends again?" Overwhelmed by nostalgia, she'd spoken without thinking. She'd missed Ace's solid presence in her day-to-day life, and although they were no longer a couple in love, it didn't mean they couldn't have a cordial relationship.

He paused a moment as if he was deep in thought. "I don't know if that's possible," he answered with a shrug. "We didn't start out as friends, Maya. From the very beginning we were two people who shared an amazing romantic connection. The first time I ever clapped eyes on you, it felt like the ground quaked underneath me. And honestly, that feeling never changed during the time we were together."

His words slammed against her chest, leaving her breathless. All this time she'd been so caught up in erasing Ace from her mind that she had forgotten how it had been between them. Electrifying. Thrilling. They had truly shared a genuine love story.

Ace quirked his mouth. "I'm not sitting around pining after you," he continued, "but that doesn't mean I want to hang out together and pretend as if we didn't once mean the world to each other."

"I don't see it as pretending," she said feebly. Suddenly, she felt like a complete idiot for thinking she could repair things so easily. There was still a wide canal standing between them that was bigger than the Yukon River.

"If you'd wanted to stay friends you wouldn't have bolted out of Alaska the way you did." His voice was curt and no-nonsense. "You ended our relationship and never said another word to me."

Ace was right. She'd been so intent on hiding her leukemia diagnosis from Ace and her parents that she hadn't wanted to face him. He'd known her so well, so much so that Maya had believed Ace would see straight through her lies. She had flown out of Owl Creek a few days later to meet with her oncologist and undergo a month of chemo treatments in Seattle. After finishing up chemo, Maya had taken classes at Seattle Pacific, taking breaks from vet school when the treatments became too intense or made her too ill. For the last phase of chemo, the treatments had been less intense, with the goal of keeping the leukemia at bay. At that point she'd been able to focus on graduating and completing all of her requirements.

Right now she had an opening to speak her truths. They had been bottled up inside her for all these years, just yearning to be released.

Please, Lord. Show me the way. Give me the courage to speak to Ace with an open heart, fearing nothing. The truth shall set me free.

"I thought it would be easier for both of us—" she began before Ace cut her off.

"What you put me through wasn't easy!" Ace jumped down from the truck and turned to face her. "Maya, it's five years too late for excuses. Back then I would have given my right arm to get an explanation from you, but now it doesn't matter. So, with all due respect, save your breath. Whatever it is, I don't need to hear it."

Ouch. Ace's sentiments cut to the bone. She should have left well enough alone and been content with their enjoying a peaceful meal together. Instead, she'd pressed it by asking for more.

"Thanks for the pizza," Ace said. "I really need to get going. C'mon, Luna." He patted his leg and she raced to his side.

Before Maya could even say good-night, Ace had turned on his boot-clad feet and strode off toward his truck. Maya sat still and watched his truck until the flash of his taillights vanished from view. *Why couldn't I have just let things be?* she asked herself. It had been foolish to push Ace. All the progress she'd made with him over the last two days had disappeared right along with Ace.

He'd made it quite clear that he didn't want anything more than a professional relationship with her and she'd gotten the message. Although it stung to be rejected by Ace, Maya realized it might be for the best. Her goal of establishing a dog rescue was mere days away from being realized. She owed Ace a debt of gratitude for taking the lead position, even though he'd been reluctant at first. Maya didn't want to jeopardize her partnership with Ace by blurring the lines between work and their personal lives.

If she made any false moves with Ace, she feared he might just abandon the job and leave her without anyone to lead her beloved Owl Creek Dog Rescue.

The following day, Ace kept his head down while working at his new place of employment. The events of last night were still weighing on his mind. He never should have stuck around for pizza with Maya. Being in such close confines with her had resulted in him letting down his guard. Their old familiar rhythms had crept back in and he'd found himself speaking about things he didn't usually discuss with anyone. And then, she'd given him the let's-be-friends line. *Friends?* After all the lost years between them? He hadn't been able to sit there and pretend as if it hadn't bothered him. Ace wasn't proud of the way he'd hightailed it away from the dog-rescue site, but he hadn't been able to stomach the idea of listening to Maya making excuses for shattering his heart.

At lunchtime, he drove to Main Street so he could take a stroll and get some fresh air. With the weather warming up, more residents were going out to lunch and socializing with friends. Although his hometown always was a social place, at times the harsh winter weather kept residents at home. He figured it would be the perfect time for him to start looking for an assistant. The pressure was on for him to bring someone on board before Friday rolled around. Ace was getting more and more excited about meeting all of the rescues. Maya had left a folder for him detailing which dogs were arriving in the first batch. So far he'd read the files for half of them. One dalmatian, two Labradors, two huskies and one terrier mix. Seeing their pictures made Ace forget all about the hassle of working with his ex. At least for a little while, he reckoned.

He was meeting up with Leo and Braden for lunch at the Snowy Owl Diner. Ace planned to ask them for suggestions about a pool of applicants for the job. Since he'd been away from Owl Creek training his sled-dog team, he wasn't in a great position to know who might be a good fit for the position. Certainly not Zach. He loudly groaned at Maya's over-the-top suggestion. She'd always been a softie for his brother, even going so far as to defend him when he got into scrapes all over town.

He couldn't blame Maya for being a good person who believed in people. Hadn't she been his biggest fan, encouraging him in his dog-sledding career more than anyone else ever had? She'd been his own personal cheering section in every race she had attended. *Go, Ace. You've got this.* He could almost hear her voice shouting at him from the crowd as she waved a Team Ace flag.

Ace parked his truck in front of Tea Time,

a local tea emporium that boasted dozens of exotic varieties. He couldn't think of the last time he'd been able to leisurely stroll down this street and absorb all of the small-town flavor. There were so many charming aspects of his hometown. The smell of chocolate hovered in the air as he walked past the North Star Chocolate Shop. One look through the shop window revealed an assortment of goodies—truffles, pecan clusters, nonpareils and so much more. Ace spotted Connor's wife, Ella, working at the counter and they cheerfully waved to one another. He resisted the temptation to pop inside, knowing he was already a few minutes late for lunch. Instead, he picked up his pace and arrived at the Snowy Owl a few minutes later.

"Hi, Ace." The petite woman who greeted him within seconds of his arrival was a welcome sight. With her café-au-lait complexion and a head of curly hair swirling about her shoulders, Piper North was as radiant as ever.

"Hey, Piper," Ace said, reaching down and hugging the lovely diner owner. "Marriage suits you. Congratulations."

"Thanks. You look pretty good yourself." She furrowed her brow. "Where've you been hiding? I heard you were back in Owl Creek, but this is the first time you've graced us with your presence at the diner."

"I've been around. Trying to keep busy and stay out of trouble," Ace said, flashing her a grin.

"Oh, I remember you and Hank getting into plenty of scrapes back in the day," she said with a shake of her head. Piper jerked her head in the direction of the back table. "Leo is here, but my husband is running late. You two should probably go ahead and order."

After thanking Piper, Ace headed toward the table and sank into the booth seat directly across from his best friend. According to the women in town, Leo was the most under-the-radar bachelor in Owl Creek. With sandy-brown hair and hazel eyes, women got weak in the knees over him. Sweet and generous, Leo tended to keep a low profile out at the Duggan family ranch. Leo had been Ace's constant companion since first grade.

The Duggan family had recently endured the loss of Leo's cousin Ethan, who'd died while serving overseas in the military. It had been particularly tragic since Ethan had just gotten engaged and was preparing to leave military service to head back to Alaska.

Leo laid down his menu on the table and

focused on Ace. "Hey there. I was beginning to wonder if you guys were going to stand me up. I've practically memorized the menu."

"No chance of that. I'm starving. Not sure about Braden since Piper suggested we go ahead and order." They both knew how busy Braden was these days with starting his sports-adventure company and helping out with Pie in the Sky, the pie business he'd created with his wife.

He quickly glanced at the menu, then pushed it aside. More times than not he ordered a salmon burger with rosemary fries and a cup of black-bean chili when he ate at the Snowy Owl. Ace knew he should probably try something new, but he was a creature of habit in most aspects of his life. It was one of the reasons he'd been having such a hard time adjusting to things after leaving the dog-sledding world. He thrived on the familiar rhythms of life.

Their server brought them waters and took their lunch order. Leo decided to order the same thing as Ace but opted for conch fritters rather than fries. The fritters had become a popular item in Owl Creek.

"So how's it going at the dog rescue? You

must be busy setting up the place," Leo said, taking a sip of his water.

"So far, so good. We have twelve dogs arriving on Friday, so that will be the true test of where we stand," Ace responded. "I need to hire an assistant, so any recommendations would be appreciated. I also need a few volunteers, but I think I might have a handle on that." Ace knew a lot of folks in town who were passionate about dogs, but none of them were available to work for him for one reason or another.

"Let me think about it. I'll try to come up with a few names for you," Leo said.

"I'd appreciate that. Getting off to a good start with the program is crucial to its success. Maya has done a really good job of getting the funding together and setting up the facilities."

Leo narrowed his gaze as he locked eyes with him. "I still can't believe you and Maya are working together." He leaned in and asked in a low voice, "Given everything that went down between you two, are you sure that's a good idea?"

"I'm not sure of anything at the moment," he answered with a sigh. "No, I'm going to take that back. I'm excited about working with rescue dogs and making an impact in their lives. That really fuels my fire, and I haven't felt excited about anything in a long time," Ace admitted. "I think I was really depressed after the accident. Training dogs was my life, and having it all come to a sudden crashing halt, no pun intended, was devastating."

"I kind of figured by the way you holed yourself up at your dad's place that you were hurting," Leo said, his tone infused with sympathy. "Believe me, I get it. Losing Ethan has been soul-crushing."

Ace sent him a sympathetic look. Ethan had been the town's golden boy and an American hero. His tragic death had sent tremors throughout town.

"So to answer your question, I refused the job offer at first because I couldn't fathom the idea of us working so closely together." Ace ran a hand over his jaw. "But, my hands were tied when Dane dropped his bombshell." Ace had already told Leo all about his dad's mortgage catastrophe. He had full confidence that he wouldn't let it slip to a single soul. In small towns, gossip tended to fly on the wind. Ace didn't want to put his dad in the uncomfortable position of being whispered about due to his financial issues.

The server returned with their meals and placed them down on the table in front of them.

"You were really in love with her," Leo said before tucking into his food. "I don't think I've ever seen anyone so besotted."

"Besotted? I don't like that word. It makes me sound like a chump." Ace dipped a few of his fries in ketchup. "That was a long time ago. I'll admit there's a bit of tension between us, but I think if we just focus on our purpose it'll be fine."

Leo made a face. In that they'd been best friends for decades, Ace knew Leo's facial expression meant something.

"What?" Ace asked. "Why'd you make that 'yeah, right' face?"

Leo lightly heaved his shoulders. "I didn't know I made one, but it seems to me that the two of you have a lot of stuff to unpack. You never really understood why Maya broke things off with you. She wasn't exactly fair to you. And now you're going to be joined at the hip with her."

Ace resisted the temptation to groan as he bit into his salmon burger. There was nothing in this world like good, Alaskan-cooked food. The Snowy Owl had always been his favorite restaurant in town, going back to when he was a kid and Piper's dad had run the place. He'd never been disappointed.

"I appreciate your being on my side," Ace said, "but I've had to learn not to dwell on the past. If I do, it'll just set me back. I'm going to give this dog rescue my all and pray for the best. It's really all I can do."

"Let me know if there's anything I can do to help," Leo said. Ace knew Leo meant it. He mentally stashed away his friend's offer for a time when he might really require it.

"You wouldn't happen to be in need of a rescue dog, would you?" Ace asked with a chuckle. "Pretty soon I'll have forty on my hands."

Leo joined in on the laughter. It seemed like old times to Ace. Both men had endured difficulties over the last few years, yet they were still standing.

"Let me think about it," Leo answered. "The ranch is pretty much a menagerie at the moment."

Just then Braden showed up at their table, with a sheepish expression stamped on his face. "Sorry, guys," he said, scooting next to

Ace in the booth seat. "I was delivering pies. We're swamped this time of the year."

"No worries," Leo reassured him. "Ace was just telling me about his new gig. He's leading up the dog-rescue project Maya created."

Braden turned to face him with a stunned expression. "No way!" he exclaimed.

Ace ran a weary hand over his face. Was this going to be the consensus of all the residents in Owl Creek every time they found out about his new role? Utter disbelief? Head-shakes and whispers? A little sigh slipped past his lips as he prepared to tell yet another person that, against his better judgment, he was now working in close proximity to his ex.

Chapter Six

Maya looked down at the sign she'd commissioned for the dog rescue. She traced the letters with her finger, pride swelling within her at the artistry and craftsmanship of the piece. The sign was rustic and beautiful. She'd called in a favor from a local woodworking friend, Russ Simpson, who'd surprised her by dropping off the sign bright and early this morning. Russ, ever grateful for her saving his pug's life last year, had done a rush job for her.

Her first instinct had been to head next door to show Ace the new sign, but things were now awkward between them. She wasn't sure if he would be receptive to any cordial overtures she made, even though this was directly related to the refuge. *This is ridiculous*, she thought. They had more matters to resolve before Friday, and avoiding each other wasn't going to cut it. A quick glance at her watch confirmed that she had some time to head over and meet with Ace before her next client arrived. With the sign tucked under her arm, Maya headed out the door toward the dog rescue. Once she was inside, Maya immediately noticed the changes Ace had made to the place.

There was a dog bed in each kennel, and on the outside front panel sat whiteboards with each dog's name, along with a space for their likes and dislikes, food allergies, medicines and feeding times.

Suddenly, Maya heard the patter of paws on the vinyl flooring. Luna was heading straight toward her with her tongue hanging out of her mouth and her tail vigorously wagging. Before she knew it, Luna was standing beside her, angling for Maya to pat her. Resistance was futile, Maya realized. Luna wasn't the type of dog a person could ignore, what with her sweet face and upbeat personality. She was such an amazing tripod. Ace soon came into view, coming out of the kitchen area with a large mug cupped in his hands.

"Hey, Ace," she greeted him. "The place looks great."

"Thanks. I didn't do much. Just a few amenities and some spit and polish. Someone anonymously dropped off some collars, toys and leashes to add to our collection." Ace smiled. "There's an assortment in every color of the rainbow."

"That's incredible. I never stop being amazed at the generosity of people in Owl Creek."

"Something tells me this is just the beginning," Ace said. "Once everyone finds out we've opened our doors, I think donations are going to be through the roof."

"From your lips to God's ears." Maya pointed toward the kennels. "These whiteboards are a great idea. It'll make it easier to keep track of each dog and their specific issues. I wish I'd thought of it myself."

"What do you have there?" Ace asked, jutting his chin toward the sign she'd propped against the wall.

She picked up the sign and showed it to Ace. "Russ did a bang-up job with the sign, didn't he?" she asked, eager to hear his opinion. His validation still meant so much to her. Ace had always had high standards, so if he gave it a thumbs-up, she knew it was perfect.

Ace studied it closely, then finally said,

"It's fantastic. The colors really pop. I can hang it up if you'd like," Ace suggested. "Just give me a few minutes, and I'll get right on it."

"Help! We need some help out here!" a high-pitched voice called from outside. Ace and Maya looked at each other, both alarmed by the cries. Seconds later, Ace rushed toward the door, with Maya at his heels. There was no question that someone was in distress. It pulsed in the air around them as the screams continued. A young woman Maya recognized from the North Star Chocolate Shop, Sierra Nielsen, was kneeling on the ground beside her vehicle. A yellow Labrador retriever was in the back seat, panting and drooling. Maya's first thought was that the canine was dehydrated and quite ill.

Sierra looked up at them as they approached. "I found her out by the woods all by herself with no collar, no identification. She's in trouble. I think she might be dying." There was a frantic energy hovering over the scene.

Maya quickly stepped forward, gently moving Sierra out of the way so she could focus on the animal. The pup's stomach was distended and heaving up and down. There was discharge seeping from her eyes and she didn't even seem to know Maya was there.

Maya turned back toward Ace. "I need some help lifting her and bringing her inside to one of the examination rooms."

Ace stepped up and leaned into the car, his movements gentle and precise as he boosted the dog into his arms. She let out a whimper, clearly in pain. Ace winced at the sound, his face reflecting his sorrow over the situation. This man lived and breathed dogs just as much as Maya did. Seeing an abandoned dog in this condition was heartbreaking. Maya ran ahead of Ace and jerked open the door. Peggy gaped at her, then stood up and came from behind her desk to help. In a flurry of activity, Maya and Peggy went ahead to the examination room, followed by Ace.

"Lay her down on the mat," Maya instructed. Ace did as she asked, then backed away to give her room to examine the dog. "Peggy, could you tell my next patient it might be a while? They can either come back later this afternoon or reschedule for tomorrow morning."

"Will do," Peggy said, walking out of the room toward the waiting area.

"Ace, would you mind seeing if Sierra is

still here? I'd like to know if she might have seen or heard anything that can trace the dog back to her owners. She's definitely not one of my patients. I think she's been abandoned, judging by her condition and matted hair."

Without saying a word, Ace hightailed it out of the exam room. Maya had the feeling he didn't want to be around a suffering dog, despite how much he adored them. She imagined it was hard for him after being in the crash, where several of his sled dogs had been injured.

Maya began her examination, keeping an eye out for confirmation of what she suspected based on the pup's symptoms. The dog's whimpering was intensifying to a point where Maya knew things were escalating fast.

Lord, please watch over this sweet pup. Make her suffering go away. Heal her as only You can.

"You're going to be all right, Daisy," she crooned, coming up with the name on the spot. She had the feeling they might never be able to find the Lab's owners, and if she was correct, the dog needed a name. Matter of fact, they would soon need numerous names. She left the room, knowing Daisy wouldn't be going anywhere in her condition.

She immediately saw Ace leaning against the wall. Luna was beside him keeping him company. It was nice to see the closeness between them. Luna had to be one of the most well-adjusted tripod dogs she'd ever known. No doubt it was due to Ace's love and attention.

"How's it going? I talked briefly to Sierra. She didn't see anything other than the dog in distress," he said, strain evident on his face. This was a part of Ace few people saw. On the surface he seemed cavalier, but the truth was he cared about things deeply.

"She's doing as well as can be expected under the circumstances. There are two things going on. She has all the symptoms of heartworm, which makes sense since her owner clearly hadn't taken care of her. Also, she's in labor, Ace."

"Labor?" he asked, his brown eyes radiating shock. "She's pregnant?"

"Yes," Maya confirmed, "and pretty sick from malnourishment and heartworm. This delivery isn't going to be easy. I'm just thankful the pups can't get heartworm in utero or during delivery. We can also make sure they're put on heartworm meds at six weeks old as a preventative. And I'm putting Daisy on medicine immediately."

"Can I help? I promise not to get in the way. I'm feeling pretty invested at the moment."

He looked a little green around the gills, and for a second she feared he might get sick. Beads of sweat were dotted on his forehead and he seemed shaky.

She appreciated the offer to help, but if he wasn't up to it, Maya understood. "Ace, how are you holding up? Are you okay?"

"I'm okay," he said. "I never wanted to see a dog suffer again the way Luna did. But here I am once again. I just need to shake it off."

Maya made a tsking sound. "It's terrible seeing such neglect in a dog, never mind a pregnant one. There's no telling how long she was out there in the woods with no food or water."

"Some people aren't fit to own dogs," Ace said forcefully, his mouth twisted in anger.

Maya had felt this way a handful of times in her career. It wasn't a good feeling, but it was a sad reality she faced in her profession. Back in California, Maya had dealt with clients who'd boarded their dogs at her vet practice and never returned to pick them up. It had been her first experience with owner neglect and it still stung. Those dogs had been her first rescues.

"You don't have to stay if you don't want to," she said, knowing he might feel more comfortable heading back to the other building.

"I want to stay," he said, locking eyes with her. She could see the determination in his eyes, and she respected his commitment to a dog he barely knew. But she wasn't surprised by his dedication. It was this very quality that she'd been searching for in the applicants to lead the dog-rescue program. Ace was right where he needed to be.

When they went back to the exam room and Maya checked in on Daisy, she discovered that her delivery was imminent. It was extremely serendipitous that Sierra had found the pregnant pup in the woods. If not, Daisy would have been facing certain death during her delivery.

Ace set up a birthing area on the ground with a mat and some old blankets. He had towels nearby for the puppies. Daisy's breathing and panting became more labored until Maya spotted the first pup coming into the world. One by one, the puppies were delivered—five in all. Ace gently used a towel to wipe the meconium off each puppy, then placed them on a blanket in a nearby box.

Maya lifted up each puppy, one at a time, and examined them. "It's pretty shocking how good they look. Their color is nice, and none of them are struggling."

"It's really amazing," Ace gushed, his face lit up with wonder. "Good job, Maya."

"Daisy did all the hard work. Dogs are incredibly resilient," Maya said, wiping her brow with her forearm. Hearing Ace's praise nearly sent her over the edge. She tried to hold it together, but a few tears slid down her cheeks. This was a moment of pure triumph and the very reason she had gone to veterinary school. Experiencing it with Ace was indescribable.

Ace was holding one of the puppies after toweling him off. He raised the pup to Maya's face, and she reached out and nuzzled it with her palm. The moment felt intimate and uplifting. She sensed Ace felt it, too. There was a lightness about him in this moment that was a big departure from his demeanor the other night. He wasn't all sharp edges. He was kinder and gentler. Just the way he was cradling the puppy in his arms brought back his tenderness. Oh, how she missed being the object of his affection. He used to make her feel as if she was the sun, moon and stars all wrapped up into one person.

"Hey. Things are stable with Daisy and her puppies. What's wrong?" he asked, worry lines creasing his forehead.

"Well, it just hit me that we've just added six more dogs to our roster," Maya said, letting out a slight laugh to mask the deep underbelly of emotion she was battling against. What was the point in Ace knowing how conflicted she was over ending things with him five years ago? It might hamper his ability to work with her and she couldn't do anything to jeopardize the dog-rescue operation. She could never get back what she'd lost with Ace. There was still a huge lie standing between them that felt like an albatross around her neck, along with the fear that her leukemia would return. Those were two huge reasons why she needed to keep Ace at arm's length and not allow herself to reminisce over their past.

Maya would just have to stuff it all down and play the role she'd assigned herself five years earlier. She couldn't allow Ace to ever find out that she'd only broken up with him because of how much she'd once loved him.

* * *

By the time Ace made it home, he was bleary-eyed. It was fine, though, since the birth of Daisy's pups had gone well. All of the puppies had survived, which was a blessing given Daisy's condition. Mother and puppies were holding their own, and according to their vet, they had a great shot at survival. At the end of the day, that's all they could hope for. A chance. He was adding Daisy and her brood to his prayers.

Watching Maya guide Daisy through a tough delivery had been amazing. There had been so many years of hard work on her part and dreaming about becoming a veterinarian. For years she'd scrimped and saved to supplement her tuition funds. Her skill and compassion had been on full display today, and even though he had nothing to do with her accomplishments, Ace felt incredibly proud of Maya.

There had been that one moment between them when he'd felt as if all the oxygen in the room had vanished. Something crackled and pulsed between them that he hadn't even wanted to acknowledge. It had been potent and powerful. And way too heady to face head-on. He hadn't stayed much longer after that encounter. The two of them being alone in a confined space could easily take them down roads they might regret.

He scooped Luna up from the passenger seat instead of letting her jump down. She was tired and he'd noticed she was wobbling more than usual. "It's okay if I carry you from time to time, girl. You're still the most independent dog I know," he crooned. Luna made him feel like an old softie. Certain animals were so defenseless, much like the dog Maya had named Daisy. All they asked for was to love and be loved. It was too bad, he thought, that humans couldn't be more like canines. He hadn't been looking for love these last few years, but he knew from past experience how wonderful it could be.

When he opened the back door, the padding of numerous paws signaled that he was about to get bombarded by his crew of dogs. Within seconds he was proven right. The dogs greeted him with so much enthusiasm that they nearly knocked him off his feet. All he could do was laugh. This was life as a dog owner of multiple canines and he loved it. "Easy there. You just saw me this morning," he said, chuckling as he lavished attention on Silky, Yukon and Denali.

Ace took out a bowl and filled it up with food, then placed it down in front of Luna. He'd discovered that the rest of the dogs had been fed based on a quick phone call he'd made earlier to his dad. Knowing that his dogs were all taken care of at the moment, Ace let out a sigh of exhaustion. He suspected this particular feeling was based on the emotional aspects of the day and watching Maya save Daisy and her litter's lives. They'd both felt so much joy at the outcome, but the delivery had been full of tension until the pups had safely arrived in good condition.

"Hey! How's it going?" Ace asked his younger brother as he headed into the kitchen to heat up some leftovers. Zach was sitting at the kitchen counter with a bowl of ramen noodles in front of him and a can of soda. With his closely shaven dark hair, angular features and lean physique, Zach didn't resemble Ace at all. He did, however, look like their mother, which always served as a reminder to Ace that he'd promised her he'd watch over Zach.

"Not good, but what do you care?" Zach muttered, shooting Ace a dirty look.

Ace stopped in his tracks and frowned at Zach. He should really ignore his self-pitying comment and make his dinner. His stomach was already starting to make rumbling noises. How many times had he fallen into Zach's trap of making him feel sorry for him? His brother really needed to grow up in a hurry.

"What's gotten into you?" Ace asked, going against his better judgment and engaging with Zach.

"Several people told me you're looking for an assistant to work with you at the dog rescue. So what about me?" Zach asked. "I don't recall you asking me if I wanted the job." His lower lip was stuck out in a pout, transporting Ace back to the days when he was a toddler. *Some things never change*, he realized. It was Zach's world and everyone else was just living in it.

"What about you?" Ace asked in a raised voice. "Dad can't even get you to help around the house without you getting an attitude. This is serious business, Zach. These rescues are coming from desperate situations and they need support and devotion and consistency."

"I could do all that!" Zach pleaded. "Give me a shot."

Ace let out a snort. "Since when?"

"Since now," he insisted. "I'm not the same person I used to be."

"Why do you want this job so badly? Aren't you working out at the factory?" Ace asked. He'd been under the impression that his brother was doing some part-time shifts at the North Star Chocolate factory. It was the biggest industry in Owl Creek, and he'd heard they paid well. Not to mention the Norths were fair-minded, good folks.

"I quit a few weeks ago." Zach hung his head. The sight of him looking so dejected smacked Ace squarely in the chest. "I could use the money. I'm trying to go back to school next year."

"Seriously? That's great," he exclaimed, trying to hide his shock. His younger brother could be overly sensitive at times so he had to play it cool. Zach had barely lasted a semester at Kenai Peninsula College until he dropped out two years ago. The truth was he'd been floundering quite a bit since their mother's death six years ago. Ace harbored a lot of guilt that he'd been too wrapped up in his own grief to help his brother find his way.

Zach swung his head up and locked gazes with Ace. "I'm trying to change. I want to be more responsible and do things the right way. Everything in my life will improve if I can get back to school and make a future for myself."

Ace knew instinctively the times when Zach was trying to scam him and this wasn't one of them. He was being sincere. Just hearing his frustration and pain gutted Ace. No matter what, Zach was family. Their mother would want Ace to do whatever he could to help him. Hadn't he promised her he would do just that?

"It's long hours. And between the two of us we'd have to manage forty dogs, plus the litter Maya delivered today and their mama. We seriously need volunteers." He let out a groan. "Rescue dogs will always need a safe place to live and we're never going to turn any dogs in need away."

"Of course not. These dogs need to be taken care of, at all costs," Zach responded.

He sent his brother a stern look. "If I give you this opportunity, Zach, you have to give it your all. I'm not kidding. These rescue dogs deserve the best of us."

"Are you giving me the position?" Ace thought Zach's jaw might drop to the floor. A nervous tic above his eyebrow was throbbing.

"I'm considering it," he said slowly.

"'Let your light so shine before men, that they may see your good works,'" Zach said, looking up at him with puppy-dog eyes. The verse from Matthew was one of Ace's favorites, and Zach knew it. Was his brother laying it on thick or being authentic? Time would tell.

"You're hired, starting bright and early tomorrow morning. On a trial basis," Ace said through clenched teeth. "One false move, and you're gone."

Zach let out a whoop of delight, then jumped up from his seat and wrapped his arms around Ace's neck. "You're the best. I won't let you down," he said as Ace untangled himself from Zach's grip.

"I'm counting on it. We don't have a lot of time before our first batch of dogs arrive on Friday, so all hands on deck."

"And I promise to give you and Maya lots of privacy," Zach said with a wink.

Ace glared at him. "One more comment like that, and you'll be fired before you start. My relationship with Maya is purely professional. Saying stuff like that is what sparks rumors."

Zach's cheeks reddened. "It won't happen again," he said, looking sheepish.

Ace turned toward the fridge and took out some leftover baked ziti he'd made a few days ago. As he zapped it in the microwave, he started to worry that he'd let his heart override his head regarding hiring Zach as his assistant. He had been so dead set against it, yet he'd given in so easily once Zach gave him a sob story. He couldn't help but recall that every time he allowed emotion to rule him he ended up regretting it. Maya's face flashed before his eyes. He'd given her the best part of himself, and it hadn't been enough. Ace had loved her in a way he hadn't thought it was possible to love. And yet…he'd put his heart out there only to have it smashed into pieces.

When would he learn to harden his heart? He was wary of being around Maya. Being in her presence today had reinforced all the reasons why he'd fallen head over heels in love with her. And it had shown him how dangerous it was to be around her. He didn't want to get burned.

Not this time, he thought. Being compassionate toward Zach was one thing. Allowing himself to fall for Maya all over again wasn't going to happen.

Chapter Seven

Don't laugh. Don't grin, either, Maya reminded herself as she stood face-to-face with Ace. Against her will, she could feel the sides of her mouth twitching in rebellion. Maybe if she didn't look at him, she wouldn't crack up. She could feel it bubbling up inside of her until she could no longer contain it. She let out a wild cackle of laughter, then clutched her belly as waves of mirth ripped through her.

"Maya, it's not that funny," Ace said, frowning at her.

She let out an indelicate snort. "Y-yes it is," she sputtered. "It's hilarious."

"You always did have a twisted sense of humor," Ace drawled.

"Y-you hired Zach after all that tough talk." She clutched her sides, unable to stop herself from full-on laughing. "Your whole attitude was anyone but Zach. You were so adamant that he was the last person we should ever employ."

Ace folded his arms across his chest and looked down at her with a scowl. "So I hired him. You know how persuasive he can be. He knows how to lay it on real thick."

"He sure knows how to play you," Maya said, holding up her fingers and rubbing them together. "Like a fiddle."

Ace rolled his eyes. "You're really having a good time with this, aren't you?"

"Okay, I'm sorry. I'm really happy you changed your mind. He kind of always felt like my little brother, too," she admitted. "And I haven't seen him much over the years. I've missed him." Back when she and Ace had been a serious couple, they'd been inseparable. They'd both been close with each other's families. Strong bonds had formed.

Her comment was a bit "open mouth, insert foot," considering the huge elephant in the room—Ace himself. She missed him, too, although she didn't have the right to say it. Not that he would be receptive to it even if she did summon the courage to tell him. She knew he'd erected a wall around himself that she couldn't penetrate. It was his defense mechanism against being hurt again. Maya knew Ace well enough to know how he operated. He reminded her of the Alaskan hermit crabs that inhabited the waters of Kachemak Bay. These crustaceans retreated into their shells as a way of protecting themselves, just like Ace did.

"So where is he?" Maya asked, eager to pivot away from her comment.

"Out back. We were thinking of making the backyard into a really cool area for the dogs to get outdoor play and exercise. If you have a minute I can show you."

"Sure thing. I'm supposed to head out to see Otis in a half hour. His dog, Winter, isn't feeling well, and he really isn't able to drive into town anymore due to his eyesight." Otis Cummings was a sweet widower who lived in a wooded area outside of town. After his wife, June, had passed away, he'd decided to bring a dog into his home.

"I'll make it quick," Ace said as he began leading her toward the back side of the building. As it came into view, Maya realized how small the area was. She'd been so busy focusing on other details about the shelter that she hadn't taken into consideration that forty dogs would need a bigger area to run around in. For what seemed like the hundredth time in the last few days, Maya thanked God for bringing Ace to the dog-rescue project.

"Hey, Maya. Long time no see," Zach said as he quickly made his way toward her. With his enthusiasm overflowing, he reached out and picked her up by the waist, then spun her around. Maya giggled at the gesture. Back when he was a little boy, Maya had spun him around in the same fashion.

"Take it easy," Ace cautioned, motioning for Zach to put her down.

"I can't believe how tall you are," she gushed once he'd placed her back down on solid ground. "You're not little anymore." She could hear a trace of sadness in her voice. She'd been gone from Owl Creek for so many years, and even though she'd been welcomed back with open arms, it felt as if she'd missed out on so much. Little Zach had grown into a young man since the days when she and Ace had been inseparable. Back then Zach had been the little brother who loved comic books and video games. Every time she'd laid eyes on him it seemed as if he'd grown a few inches.

"Thanks for letting me work here," Zach

said with a grin. "I'm looking forward to it. A love of dogs runs through my veins."

"You're right about that." Maya noticed Ace seemed pretty pleased at the comment. A smile played at the sides of his mouth.

"I was just showing Maya where we think we can expand," Ace explained. He pointed toward the area where the fencing ended. "Zach and I can extend the fenced-in area, thereby increasing the overall space for the dogs. We just need to know the boundaries of the property so we know how far we can go. If it's okay with you, that is."

She quickly pointed out the boundary lines for the property in order to reassure Ace that he had plenty of land to work with.

Maya could easily imagine a larger outside area for the dogs. It would be wonderful to see them run and play outdoors in all types of Alaskan weather. Now that spring had officially sprung in Owl Creek, there would be less snow and warmer temperatures.

"Ace, you don't need my permission to make changes here. You're in charge of the dog rescue… I trust you."

She met Ace's gaze. Surprise flared in his eyes. "I appreciate it," he said. "We can get materials pretty cheap and we'll do the work ourselves."

"Will it be done by Friday?" she asked, knowing it was a long shot.

"We'll do our best, won't we, Zach?" Ace asked, swinging his gaze toward his brother, who flashed Maya a thumbs-up sign.

"We've got this, Maya," he said. "The Owl Creek Dog Rescue is going to be the most happening place in town." His words caused both Ace and Maya to laugh. Just thinking about a dog rescue being a trendy hangout spot was pretty hilarious.

"As long as we find forever homes for these animals, it's fine by me," Maya said. It was her most heartfelt wish. This mission to support rescue dogs had been imprinted on her heart for such a long time. She would never have the words to fully express what it meant to her to see it come to fruition.

A sudden wave of nausea washed over her, and she clutched her midsection. She felt clammy all over. She could feel moisture pooling on her neck and forehead. Maya began fanning her face in the hopes that it would make her feel less flushed. It happened so quickly that it took her breath away.

"Are you okay?" Ace asked, concern etched on his face. "You don't look so good."

As she opened her mouth to answer, she swayed, feeling unsteady on her feet. Ace was right there to catch her, grabbing her by her elbow and forearm.

"I—I don't know," she answered. "I feel weak all of a sudden."

"Do you need some water?" Zach asked. "Let me go get some for you." Zach took off running toward the building.

Ace leaned down and scooped her up in his arms despite her feebly telling him it wasn't necessary. "I think we need to go inside and let you sit down," Ace said in a firm voice. "You might be dehydrated."

"I—I'm fine," she said, trying to get her bearings. She still felt woozy and a bit nauseous. She didn't even have strength at the moment to fight Ace. What was going on with her?

Ace managed to open the door while still cradling her against his chest. Once he got her inside, he headed toward the kitchen and gently placed her in a wooden chair. Zach unscrewed the top of a bottle of water and extended it toward Maya. She gratefully accepted the drink and began guzzling it down.

"Feel any better?" Ace asked anxiously. He was standing so close to her chair that she could hear the sound of his ragged breathing.

"I really should get going so I'm not late for my appointment with Otis." She stood up, wincing as another wave of nausea hit her. She sank back down onto the chair.

"Maya, you're in no condition to drive out to Otis's place," Ace cautioned. "God forbid you get into an accident in your condition."

"I can't leave Otis high and dry. He's counting on me." Emotion threatened to overtake her. "He's all alone now that June's passed away. I think he's lonely."

Ace bit his lip. "I know you don't want to disappoint him, but if you're not well, Maya, it doesn't make sense to go all the way over there."

Maya knew Ace was right. Whatever was going on with her hadn't fully subsided. The water had helped to hydrate her, but driving on snowy, winding roads could be challenging.

"Can you drive me out there, Ace? We don't have to stay long. I just need to check out Winter and spend a little time with her." Maya shot him a pleading look. "I'm feeling a little better already."

"I can hold the fort down and keep an eye on Luna," Zach suggested. "Maybe I can even get started on the fencing materials."

Maya knew Ace was mulling it over in his mind. It was easy for her to spot the look of introspection on his face. She crossed her hands prayerfully.

Ace let out a groan of surrender. "Okay, I'll take you out to Otis's place, but we can't spend all day there. We're up to our elbows in things to finish around here."

Maya let out a little whoop of joy. As a veterinarian, keeping promises meant everything to her. Otis and Winter were two of her favorite clients, and it wouldn't feel right to bail on them, even if she had a pretty good reason. "Thank you so much, Ace. Otis will be so thrilled to see us." Her first instinct had been to throw her arms around him and give him a tight hug, but she knew that wouldn't have been the right move. *Those days are gone*, she realized. Even though she was finding out that old habits were hard to break.

Now, they had a fledgling partnership that might not withstand the test of time. She didn't know long they could coexist with tensions simmering between them.

After grabbing a bag of supplies and medication from her office, Maya made her way out front, where Ace was waiting. He moved toward his truck and opened the front passenger door, then helped her step up and into the vehicle. Although she appreciated the gesture, she was almost feeling back to normal. The strange episode had passed, but it left her unsettled.

A trickle of fear ran through her that she couldn't seem to shake off. For so long now she'd been afraid of her leukemia coming back. And now, based on the symptoms she'd experienced this morning, she actually had something tangible to be frightened about.

Otis lived about ten minutes from town in a rustic log cabin nestled against the foothills of the mountains. This was the bucolic Alaska that folks dreamed about—bald eagles soaring in the sky, snow-covered Sitka spruce trees and moose roaming the landscape. Ace loved driving to the outskirts of Owl Creek and absorbing all the wonders of the area. Being alone in his truck with Maya brought back a host of memories. Because of the close confines of the interior, the flowery scent that clung to Maya quickly rose to his nostrils. For the life of him, he couldn't think of anything to say to Maya in order to fill up the silence. There was something about the two of them being in his truck that felt intimate. And he wasn't sure he could handle it. If anyone had told him a few weeks ago that he would be sitting here with Maya, he wouldn't have believed it. Little by little she was chipping away at his defenses, and it worried him. Instead of remembering how she'd ended things between them without any real explanation, he found himself recalling all the good times they'd shared. Even though he projected a tough image, he didn't have much of a defense to put up against Maya. Or the feelings she dredged up in him.

Lord, let me be stronger.

Maybe it had been better when he'd hardened his heart against her. It had been easier, that was for sure.

When he reached to turn on the radio, his arm brushed against hers. It was the simplest of movements, yet to Ace it felt like a shock to the system. He was so aware of Maya, so attracted to her despite their fractured past. *Focus on something else other than Maya*, he told himself. He tried to focus on the trees, the weather, the melting snow. Anything but the lady sitting next to him!

"It's been a long time since I've seen Otis," Ace admitted. "I feel bad that I haven't checked in on him since I've been back."

"You need to cut yourself some slack, Ace," Maya said. "The Iditarod crash was traumatic, not just for Luna and your other dogs, but for you as well."

He cast a quick glance in her direction. "Thanks for trying to let me off the hook, but I was too busy licking my wounds to think about Otis. His situation is so similar to my dad's," Ace said. "They both lost long-term spouses. It's a hard road to travel."

"I know. June and Otis were always joined at the hip. It's a bit jarring to see him alone. But I know he'll get such a kick out of seeing you, Ace." Maya's encouragement made him grin. Maybe the folks here in town didn't view him in a bad light after all.

As they rounded a bend in the road the mountains, majestic and rugged, rose up to greet them. They turned down a tree-lined dirt road just before Otis's cabin came into view. The house looked cozy despite its slightly weather-beaten appearance. Alaskan winters were rough on homes, and Ace had the sneaking suspicion that the exterior of his house hadn't been a top priority for Otis. He made a mental note to come back out here with some paint and a power washer to fix the place up. It was the least he could do, after all of Otis's kindnesses through the years.

They walked up to the door and Maya gently knocked on it. A beautiful lavender-and-herb wreath with the word *Welcome* met them.

Otis answered right away, greeting them effusively. He heartily clapped Ace on the back. "If it isn't my favorite dog musher. You're a sight for sore eyes, Ace."

"Otis. I've missed you," Ace said, leaning in for a hug.

"I'm glad you're back in Owl Creek, but I'm sorry about the Iditarod accident. You really put our little town on the map, just like your dad and grandpop." He grinned at Ace. "What I'm trying to say is that you did us proud. Win or lose, Ace Reynolds, it's an honor and a privilege to say you're from my hometown."

"I appreciate hearing that," Ace said. "I really do." Something lifted off his shoulders at hearing Otis's warm sentiments. A part of him had been under the belief that he'd shamed himself, his family and the entire town of Owl Creek by ending his career as a professional dog musher. The crash had been his fault. It was the reason why he'd been living like a hermit. He was carrying around a feeling deep in his soul that he'd dishonored himself by not being able to push past the devastating accident and continue his career. By telling Ace he was still proud of him, Otis had given him a gift he hadn't even realized he needed until this very moment.

"Where's my patient?" Maya asked, looking around the immediate area.

Otis scrunched up his face. "Well, she's been feeling poorly so she doesn't venture far from her dog bed." He beckoned them to follow him as he walked toward the living room. It was a small room bursting with glimpses of Otis's life. There were black-and-white pictures of him and June decorating the wall, along with family photos of his kids and grands. Ace couldn't believe his eyes when he spotted a picture of him and Otis from the day he'd won his first Iditarod. It warmed his heart to remember how Otis had traveled to Nome in order to see him cross the finish line. He hadn't just been there as a fan, Ace realized. He'd been there as a friend.

"Hey, Winter, girl," Maya crooned as she

bent down to pat the dog who was curled up with a blanket and a chew toy in her bed.

Winter, Otis's one-year-old Siberian husky, was a gorgeous dog. She reminded Ace of his sled dogs. At the moment, she seemed somewhat listless. She hadn't raised herself up from her bed to greet them, which was unusual for young huskies. They were incredibly curious and energetic dogs.

Maya looked up at Otis. "Can you tell me her symptoms again?"

"Let's see… For the past few days she's been sluggish, and she isn't very interested in eating much which is odd for Winter. She's vomited a few times and is making groaning noises as if she's in pain."

Maya's expression was a perfect mix of caring and concern. She was calm and unflappable. And Otis seemed to be comforted by her reassuring manner. "I'm going to examine Winter. Hopefully that will give me some idea of what's ailing her."

Otis shifted from one foot to the other. He couldn't seem to stand still. Ace felt compassion for him. He imagined that living alone out here in the woods was less lonely with Winter by his side.

"My friend Birdie suggested her stomach

might have flipped." Otis's lips were trembling. All of a sudden he seemed very vulnerable. "She said it happened to one of her dogs years ago."

"Let's not let our minds go there just yet," Maya advised, sending Otis an encouraging smile. "It can be scary when we hear about serious dog issues. That's why I tell all my clients not to look up symptoms."

Ace felt himself tensing up. He knew stomach flipping in dogs was a serious matter and involved surgery. Tad James, one of his racing buddies, had dealt with it a few years ago with his malamute. It could potentially be fatal. He prayed it wasn't anything serious.

Lord, please don't let Otis lose Winter. He's a good man, and he's already lost so much.

They both watched as Maya placed her hands on Winter's stomach and began feeling around her abdomen. A few times the dog let out a whimper. For the next ten minutes, Maya examined her as Otis and Ace looked on. Otis displayed all the nervousness of an expectant father awaiting the birth of a newborn.

"Otis, I don't think Winter's stomach has flipped for a variety of reasons. You said earlier she'd vomited. Most times if a dog's stomach has flipped, they will retch without anything coming up. Also, her stomach is making rumbling noises, but it's not distended or swollen, so that's good news." She stood up and turned toward Otis. "I think she either has a stomach virus or has gotten into something she shouldn't have. This time of year, with the harsh weather easing up, it's not unusual for dogs to go exploring and getting into things."

"Oh, that's a relief," Otis said, his shoulders immediately relaxing.

"I'm going to give you some medicine for her. It should help with her symptoms. With regards to her meals, you should stick to a rice-and-chicken diet, along with broth if you have it. I expect she'll be back to her usual self in a few days," Maya said, reaching out and squeezing Otis's hand. She rummaged around in her bag and pulled out a bottle of pills. "Here you go. This way you won't have to leave Winter to go into town."

"I'm mighty grateful for everything," Otis said, taking the medicine from Maya. "So how about a glass of iced tea and some slices of my mixed-berry pie?" Otis asked, rubbing his hands together. Ace sensed he was happy to have company. Being so far removed from town, along with his fading eyesight, limited his options for social interactions.

According to Maya, Otis was an incredible baker, and he worked for Pie in the Sky, Piper's thriving pie business. Ace thought it was fantastic that he'd found something so wonderful to fill his time with in his older years.

"I'd love a slice," Ace said, quick to take up Otis on his offer. They followed Otis into the kitchen. "I always resist buying a whole pie because it's way too tempting for my dad. He has to be careful with his sugar levels due to his diabetes."

"Now, that's something for us to think about," Otis said with a nod as he pulled out a pie and began slicing it. "A low-sugar pie. I'm going to run it by Piper and see what she says."

Otis placed slices on three plates, then slid two of them across the table before reaching into the fridge and pulling out a pitcher of iced tea. Maya had helped him out by taking three tall glasses from the cupboard and putting them on the table so Otis could fill them up. Once he was finished, Otis sat down as they all dug into the pie.

The moment the flavors hit his tongue, Ace let out a moan of appreciation. "This is terrific, Otis. It's no small wonder why these pies are in demand."

"Mmm," Maya said. "This might be my new favorite. I taste a lot of different berries, but you don't have to tell me which ones you used. I imagine it might be a secret recipe." Ace felt a stirring inside of him at the sight of Maya's beautiful face lit up as she talked to Otis. More and more he was finding it difficult to view Maya in a purely professional light. It was the very reason why he'd rejected her job offer when she had first made it. If it hadn't been for financial desperation, he wouldn't even be here right now. He had to begrudgingly admit that it felt nice to visit with Otis.

"Not much of a secret," Otis said with a chuckle. "Blueberry, raspberry and rhubarb." A huge grin stretched out across his face. "It was June's favorite."

"Well, it's a fabulous mix," Maya gushed as she ate another bite.

"So I heard the shelter is opening soon. How's everything going?" Otis asked.

"So far, so good," Ace answered. "My brother, Zach, is helping me get things ready for Friday, which is when twelve of our dogs arrive." His mood lightened just talking about the shelter. "In case you can't tell, I'm bursting with excitement to meet them."

"You're not the only one," Maya added. "I can hardly stop thinking about greeting them and getting acquainted. And, most importantly, finding homes for them."

"I'd take one if I could, but Winter here keeps me on my toes as it is," Otis explained. He popped another forkful of pie in his mouth.

"We're hoping that the community responds well to the opening of the shelter and steps in to support this project with donations," Ace said. Although he hadn't discussed it much with Maya, the money from the grants wouldn't completely cover all areas of the dog rescue in addition to salaries. At some point, there needed to be enough money coming in to support the operations of the shelter.

Otis nodded his head. "You all ought to think about setting up a booth at the Spring Fling festival. You could ask folks to fill out cards with pledges for the rescue."

"Otis, that's a fantastic idea," Maya said. "We were given grants but those are going toward salaries and medication and items for the rescue. It doesn't leave us with much of a cushion."

"We could even bring a few of the dogs to highlight adoptions. People can adopt on the spot if they fill out the paperwork and pay the fee," Ace said. His mind was whirling with the possibilities. Otis had given them a really solid idea.

The Spring Fling was an annual town event held at the beginning of the spring season. It always had a huge turnout from the townsfolk.

Otis interrupted his thoughts when he said, "I don't want to put you on the spot, but seeing the two of you together took me back a few years. You were the 'It' couple of Owl Creek if I remember correctly."

Ace nearly choked on his iced tea. It was such a random comment from Otis, one that put him and Maya under the microscope.

"That was a long time ago," Maya murmured, avoiding eye contact with Ace. For some reason it made him bristle, as if she was still avoiding all aspects of what they'd once meant to one another. Clearly, his feelings had been one-sided. What a fool he'd been to have ever thought they had a shot at a future together.

"For the life of me, I never understood why

the two of you broke up," Otis continued, his eyebrows knit together in a frown.

"You're not the only one. I was about to pop the question," Ace quipped. The words flew out of his mouth before he could rein them back in. This, he thought, was the problem with being in a relaxed atmosphere. He didn't have his wall up, as he usually did.

Maya's jaw dropped. She looked at him with wide, startled eyes.

Otis looked back and forth between them, then bit his lip. "Sorry for talking out of turn. I've clearly opened up a can of worms."

"No need to apologize, Otis. I hate to say it, but we really should be getting back," Ace said, looking at his watch. He stood up from the table. "We're in crunch time with getting the rescue's doors opened for these pups."

Maya followed his lead and stood up. "Thanks for the delicious pie, Otis. Give me a call if Winter's not getting better. I'll check in with you in a few days."

Otis walked them to the door and waved enthusiastically from his front steps as they drove away. This time the ride was filled with more tension than he'd thought possible.

Had he hurt her feelings by telling the truth about being blindsided by her? Or maybe his comment about the marriage proposal had shocked her into silence. Perhaps he'd been playing Mr. Nice Guy too much lately. In a way it felt nice to get a few things off his chest, even if his timing had been all wrong.

"Is it true what you said back there?" Maya asked in a soft voice.

He didn't bother pretending he didn't know what she was talking about. It hovered in the air between them like an electric current. "Yes, it's true. I had the ring and everything," he admitted, feeling foolish all over again for reading things so wrong between them. While Ace had been planning their future, Maya had been figuring out an exit plan. No matter what he tried to tell himself, it still stung.

He felt her gaze on him, but he kept his eyes on the road. "Ace, I—I'm so sorry. I know that I must've hurt you terribly," Maya said. The one thing he hated the most was pity. It was another reason he'd been lying low in town. All the empathetic looks and glances from the townsfolk regarding the Iditarod crash, as if he was the world's biggest failure for dropping out of the race and messing up so royally.

"Please don't feel sorry for me, Maya. It's

not as if I didn't quickly realize what a mistake it would have been if we'd gotten engaged." He let out a hollow laugh. "You and I weren't built to last. If I know anything in this world, I know that."

Maya didn't respond, and Ace didn't dare look at her. He couldn't bear to see confirmation on her face that she pitied him. He'd gone through a lot over the last number of years, and despite being at rock bottom on several occasions, he'd pushed past all of it.

But something told him that seeing a look of sympathy emanating from Maya's soulful brown eyes might just break him.

Chapter Eight

The following day, Maya found herself knee-deep in work. Between performing two minor surgeries on cats, helping to rescue a foal stuck in the ice on Kachemak Bay and fixing up a dog who had ended up full of quills after a run-in with a porcupine, she was happy to sign off for the day. She was beginning to feel that a veterinarian's job was never truly done. Bringing on another vet to the practice couldn't happen soon enough.

Later, after meeting up for dinner with Florence at her family's ranch, she would head back to her clinic to check in on the Labrador puppies and their mama.

As Maya pulled past the huge iron gates of the Double D Ranch, she took in the expansive property stretching out before her. The Duggans' land stretched out across several hundred acres. As she drove closer to the homestead, Maya spotted horses cantering around their enclosure and calves in the snow-covered field.

When she was six years old, Florence's mother, Renata, had married Patrick Duggan, owner of the ranch. Florence and her kids lived out here with her mother, stepfather and other members of the Duggan family. As her friend often said, it was a great place to raise her boys. The Double D Ranch had been in the Duggan family for generations, and even though Florence wasn't a Duggan by birth, she'd been accepted into the family as one of their own. Patrick's nephew Leo had been best friends with Ace since they were small.

It had been a long and exhausting day but Maya had promised to come out to the ranch to have an early dinner with Florence. Because she was a single mother of twins, Florence found it easier to make dinner at the ranch and host her friends there. Even though she was bone-tired, Maya believed that a promise was a promise. Florence was the type of friend she would go to the ends of the earth for, mainly because her friend had shown her that type of dedication. Maya knew things weren't easy for her as a single mother of twin boys.

As she parked and exited her truck, Maya's gaze swept over the huge, multilevel home that boasted seven bedrooms and an equal number of bathrooms. Inside, high, timbered ceilings and tall, full windows gave the house an airy, wide-open feeling. Patrick's great-grandfather had built the home, which had been added to and updated over the years.

Maya knocked on the front door. Within seconds it swung open to reveal Florence standing on the threshold. She was dressed casually in a pair of slim-fitting jeans and a long-sleeved, olive-colored top.

"Hey there, Doc. Thanks for coming out here," Florence said, warmly greeting her at the door. "It's been a while since we met up for dinner."

"Thanks for the invite." Maya looked around as she stepped inside. "It's awfully quiet in here. Where are the twins?"

"Mama and Patrick are watching them. They took them for a drive around the property. A cat had a litter of kittens they're taking a peek at."

"I'm glad you're getting a little break,"

Maya said. "I know it's not easy doing it all on your own, but you're an amazing mom."

Florence leaned in and hugged her. "Maya, you're incredibly sweet. Let's go sit down in the kitchen and get comfortable. The food is almost ready."

Maya followed Florence into the spacious all-white kitchen, where they sat down and talked while the chicken marsala continued to cook. She couldn't wait to talk to her best friend about Ace. Just when she thought she and Ace could coexist in a professional way, the past came roaring back to complicate things.

She didn't hesitate to bring up the matter with her best friend. "Ace dropped a bombshell yesterday when we paid a house call to Otis."

"Okay. Don't keep me waiting in suspense," Florence said, leaning across the table. "What did he say?"

Maya had the feeling Florence would be as shocked as she'd been. "Ace blurted out in front of Otis that he was going to ask me to marry him before we broke up."

Florence let out a little shriek. "Are you serious? And you never had any inkling he was headed in that direction?"

Maya shook her head. "We were getting serious, but we never talked about taking such a big step. I have to admit, I thought about it from time to time, wondering what our wedding would be like and how he would ask me."

Florence held up her finger. "One moment while I take the food out of the oven." Florence served up two portions, then placed the dishes on the table, followed by a salad and Italian bread. She poured them each a glass of lemonade before sitting back down. After joining their hands and praying over their meal, they both dug in and ate in companionable silence.

"This is terrific," Maya said as she finished the last of her chicken. "I wish that I could cook like this." Maya wasn't an awful cook, but she certainly couldn't whip up meals like this one.

"Thanks. Now, back to what we were talking about. If I'm being completely honest, I thought you and Ace were close to an engagement," Florence admitted. "You really seemed to be so in love with one another."

Moisture stung her eyes. Thinking about the emotional trauma of her leukemia diagnosis and losing the man she'd loved caused

her emotions to bubble over. In hindsight, it
didn't seem like a well-thought-out decision,
but she'd been in a terrible headspace back
then. "That's why I ended things with him,
Florence. I honestly wasn't sure if I was going
to make it through the leukemia, and I didn't
want to put him through that trauma. I knew
what it felt like to lose someone I loved and
so did he."

"I know how much you were hurting back
then. It must've been painful for Ace to be
on the cusp of such a big moment only to get
broken up with by the woman he loved," Florence said, quirking her mouth. "That's really
tough. It would bring anyone to their knees."

"He was definitely hurt when I ended
things, but Ace has a habit of hiding his emotions. He made it seem back then as if he
just picked himself up, dusted himself off
and went on living just fine. At least that's
how it seemed to me." At the time she had
been slightly hurt at the idea that he'd gotten
over their relationship so quickly. But now,
upon further reflection, it seemed as if Ace
had simply been really good at shuttering his
feelings.

"Leo didn't betray any confidences, but he
did mention once that Ace was really torn

apart by the way things went down between you," Florence said. She shrugged. "I think he was confused and a bit blindsided."

"I don't blame him," Maya said. It was horrible knowing she'd wounded Ace. And now that she knew he'd been on the verge of proposing marriage, she felt even worse. It made her wonder if she'd done the wrong thing. The truth was, if Ace had asked her to marry him she couldn't have accepted his proposal in good conscience. The leukemia diagnosis would have been hanging over her head like a dark cloud.

And now, her fears about being sick again were ramping up due to the episode she'd suffered yesterday. She should have immediately contacted her current oncology doctor in California and discussed her symptoms with her. It was a terrible feeling to believe she might be seriously ill. She could feel the pressure of the situation affecting her state of mind. Her nerves were on edge.

She just needed to confide in someone instead of allowing fear to fester inside of her. Since Florence knew her leukemia history, she was the obvious choice.

"I—I wasn't feeling well yesterday, Florence," Maya confessed. "It's really messing with me. You know I've always been afraid of the leukemia coming back."

"Oh, Maya. I know how frightening it must be to feel ill after all you've been through. I'm so sorry." Florence was such a nurturing person. It felt soothing simply talking to her.

"Maybe it's just stress," she hedged. "There's such a learning curve with taking over the practice it exhausts me. And with the dog rescue opening, I'm feeling a bit run-down."

"I agree you have a lot of fires burning, but why not ease your mind by having Rachel check you out?" Florence was gazing at her with an intensity Maya couldn't ignore. She wasn't going to let this go.

Rachel Lawson was a nurse married to a local pilot, Gabriel Lawson. They'd all grown up together and Maya knew Rachel was an amazing practitioner as well as being a phenomenal individual. She trusted her medical expertise.

Maya knew her reservations revolved around the fear of hearing bad news.

"Go see Rachel, Maya. She's wonderful," Florence said in an encouraging tone. "She'll put you at ease. Have her run some tests and it will reassure you when they come back as normal."

But what if the tests showed the leukemia was back? Maya couldn't even imagine going through that nightmare all over again. Maybe she did need to reach out to Rachel and find out what was going on before she let herself get into a negative mindset.

Just when Maya opened her mouth to tell Florence she would call Rachel, the sound of running feet heralded the arrival of her friend's twins. As the blond boys toddled into the kitchen and made a beeline toward Florence, Maya's heart threatened to crack wide open. Although she'd always dreamed of one day having children of her own, she worried it might not ever happen due to her chemotherapy treatments. She was open to the idea of adoption, especially since there were so many kids in the system who needed homes. Maya didn't need to give birth to a child to make it her own.

If her worst fears were realized about her health, Maya might never get the opportunity to become a mother.

Ace had to give it to Zach. He wasn't half bad as an assistant. So far he'd completed all the tasks Ace had given him, as well as initiating a few on his own. He hadn't complained once and he had no problem with the long hours. Ace was still keeping his eye on him, though. Getting the dog rescue off to a good start was imperative. Nothing or nobody was going to get in the way of a successful launch. He looked over at his brother. He was listing all the dogs' names on their individual whiteboards, along with their medications and breed. Ace realized he needed to cut him some slack. So he'd made a few youthful mistakes. It wasn't his place to judge him.

Blue liked to remind Ace that he had a tendency not to afford people second chances. He was beginning to realize his dad might be right. His thoughts immediately turned to Maya. She was one of the main reasons he was mistrustful. Being hurt by someone wasn't a great excuse, but it was the truth. Because of her, he'd developed a thick outer shell.

"Zach, why don't you head home? I can finish up and we can start bright and early tomorrow morning."

"Are you sure?" Zach asked. "I don't mind staying."

"I'm sure," Ace said with a nod. "I think we're in good shape to open up on Friday."

They'd completed the fencing earlier today with the help of some local friends. Ace grinned. Just the idea of welcoming the first of the rescue dogs made him want to celebrate.

"Okay," Zach said, wiping his brow with his forearm. "I can take Luna home and get her fed. She's probably missing the rest of the dogs," he said, nuzzling her head and getting an enthusiastic tail wag in return.

"Thanks, Zach. By the way, you're doing a great job."

Zach gaped at him. "Seriously?" he asked, uncertainty laced in his voice.

"One hundred percent," Ace said, feeling a little hitch in his heart at the smile breaking out on his brother's face. He needed to validate him more, he realized. Build him up instead of waiting for him to fail. His mother's voice rang out in his head. *You're his big brother, Ace. He looks to you for guidance. Don't let him stumble around in the dark.*

"Good to hear," Zach said, grinning. "By the way, Dad told me how you saved the house from being sold out from under him. I really respect what you did. It says a lot about who you are as a person. I know you thought that you let us down when you exited the Iditarod, but you never have…not once."

Ace felt his chest tightening with emotion. What he'd done for his father had been instinctual, and he hadn't ever wanted to be hailed as a hero for doing the right thing. It would have broken Ace's heart to see Blue lose their family home. However, hearing his little brother speak so highly of him hit Ace squarely in the chest. He cleared his throat and said, "I appreciate hearing that more than you can imagine."

Zach smiled at him. "See you at home. Come on, Luna. Let's go."

With one last look in Ace's direction, Luna followed Zach out of the building. A few minutes later he heard the roar of tires as they headed out of the lot. Ace busied himself in the kitchen making sure there was enough dog food in the cupboard, along with training treats. He'd purchased some fresh vegetables to add to the dogs' food. Not all of them would appreciate the veggies, but it was an additional nutrient to add to their diets.

Ace was so engrossed in his task that he didn't even hear approaching footsteps until Maya was standing right beside him.

When she uttered his name, it completely startled him.

"Sorry for disturbing you, Ace. I saw the light on and decided to come over."

"No worries. I was in the zone going over the feeding schedule. I'm surprised I didn't hear you come in."

He was startled to see her, considering he'd spotted her leaving the clinic hours earlier. He'd figured she was heading out for an early dinner date or running some errands. Ace didn't like thinking about Maya dating anyone. Just the thought of it made his stomach twist. It was a stunning realization considering they hadn't been together in such a long time. And he had no idea if it was simply irritation that she'd possibly moved on while he'd been stuck in limbo.

She shoved her hands in her pockets. "I was going to give you an update on the pups. Actually, if you want to come over to the clinic you can get a peek. But, if you're busy…" Her words trailed off.

She wasn't looking him in the eye, and he had to wonder if it was because of their ride back from seeing Otis yesterday. He'd been a bit harsh with his comments and she'd responded with silence, not uttering a single word to him until they reached the clinic, when she'd thanked him for driving her to see Otis. Although he'd meant what he said, Ace regretted his delivery. By the way Maya had withdrawn into herself, he knew he'd hurt her. It didn't make him feel very good about himself. Sometimes he felt like a teapot on a stove ready to boil over. It was the result of five years of not being given any answers or true closure. Pretending everything was fine had never been his strong suit.

"I've been wondering about the puppies and how they're doing," he admitted. "And I'd love to see them."

"Well, then let's head over," Maya said, turning toward the door. Ace trailed behind her, marveling at the brilliant pink moon hanging high in the sky. Maya looked up at the night sky as well, stopping in her tracks to do so. She let out a gasp. "It's gorgeous. I didn't even notice it earlier."

"Hard not to notice a moon like this one," Ace said, his tone teasing. "My mother used to call it a blushing moon. The most romantic one of all according to her."

"I've never heard it called that before," Maya murmured before looking away and continuing to walk toward the building. When they entered the clinic, Maya led him to a room where Daisy and her puppies had been set up in a cozy pen. The babies were nestled up together in a tight-knit group. Daisy was sleeping on the other side of the enclosure.

"Aww. They look great," Ace said, going down on his haunches to get a better look. Three of the puppies were yellow, while two were chocolate.

"They really are wonderful," Maya said, her face beaming with pleasure. "God was really watching out for all of them. Daisy really pulled it off, as sick as she is. And she's even nursing them."

"Is it possible that they've gotten bigger in only a short time?" Ace asked as a feeling of wonder spread through his chest.

"That's generally what they do," Maya answered.

"Oh, you've got jokes," Ace drawled, letting out a chuckle as their eyes met.

He enjoyed lighthearted moments with her. It almost made him forget about the tension that always tended to crop up when they were together. Perhaps their mutual love of dogs was the thing that would create a sense of peace between them.

Maya picked up one of the pups and handed it to Ace. "This is the runt of the litter."

Ace took the chocolate-colored pup and cradled it against his chest. Holding such a tiny helpless puppy stirred up feelings of protectiveness in him. They were completely innocent. The fact that human beings didn't honor their promises to their canine friends was heartbreaking.

"Have you named him yet?" Ace loved naming dogs. It had been one of the best parts of compiling a sled-dog team. He'd had a lot of fun with selecting cool names that fit the individual dogs. He missed the sled dogs that he'd loaned out to his close dog-musher buddies. Ace knew without a single doubt that his friends were taking good care of them. Things wouldn't feel complete until he reunited with all of his canines.

Maya shook her head. "Nope. He doesn't have a name. I'll give you the honors since you helped with the delivery."

"That's sweet considering I didn't really do anything."

"You did enough, and I appreciate it." Sincerity rang out in Maya's voice and it humbled him. Even when he acted like a jerk, she still continued to treat him with kindness.

"Frisco. I'd like to name him Frisco," Ace said, trailing his thumb against the puppy's forehead. It was a solid name for a pup who had pluck and grit. He was a survivor, much like Luna.

"I like that name. It suits him," Maya said, reaching out and running her palm over Frisco's head. Their hands brushed against each other, sending a tremor straight through him.

Maya was standing so close to him he could see the tiny, almost imperceptible freckles high up on her cheekbones. Looking into her eyes always made him feel as if he could tumble headlong into their depths. His gaze swung to her lips. They were full and perfectly shaped. At the moment, they were drawing him in and making him think about all the times he'd kissed her and what it would be like to kiss her again.

As the thought crossed his mind, he handed Frisco to Maya and took a step back. Being alone with Maya always seemed to be problematic. If there wasn't some sort of conflict brewing, he was battling a raging attraction that always sparked between them. It made him feel as if he had no idea what he was doing. He'd been so confident that he could draw a line in the sand between them, but it wasn't quite working out that way.

Kissing Maya was a terrible idea. It would be like walking down a dark and winding road wearing a blindfold. He'd already made a colossal fool of himself over her in the past. At this point, a kiss could jeopardize their working relationship. Ace couldn't deny the fact that he still harbored resentment against Maya for unceremoniously breaking up with him and shattering his heart in the process. It still baffled him. It had never made sense. But, he'd still been forced to accept it and move on with his life.

He needed to do what he'd successfully done for the last five years—ignore his feelings and put them under lock and key. *Be strong. Don't get tripped up by the past. Keep pushing forward*, he reminded himself.

"Well, thanks for letting me see the litter. And for giving me naming rights," Ace said. "I need to get some rest before tomorrow. It's our last day to get everything settled before Friday."

"You're welcome to come over anytime." She let out a chuckle. "Not that you'll have any free time with the dogs arriving soon. It just won't be *paw*-sible."

Ace tried not to laugh, but Maya's joke was so corny he just couldn't help himself. "That's really bad, Maya, but I'll forgive you a little doggy humor. Good night."

"'Night, Ace," Maya said, sounding way more untroubled than he felt. He watched as she pressed a kiss on Frisco's temple before placing him back down in the pen with his siblings.

Did she have any inkling that he'd almost kissed her? He couldn't help but wonder.

Ace headed out into the night, stopping to lock up the shelter before heading to his truck. As he drove away from Maya and the clinic, Ace turned the radio up to full volume in order to block out his chaotic thoughts. His head was all over the place. One moment he wanted to kiss her, while the next he felt the urge to head for the hills.

Every time he tried to tell himself not to get sucked in by Maya, he found himself getting pulled deeper and deeper into her world. Something was nagging at him and he couldn't let it go. Perhaps on a subconscious level he'd taken the job in order to be around Maya. There were still so many unanswered questions about their breakup that lingered. Surely, after all this time it shouldn't still bother him as it did. The fact that he still thought about it worried him.

Chapter Nine

By the time Friday rolled around, Ace and Zach had checked off every single item on their to-do list. The shelter was in impeccable condition. Ace kept looking at his watch to check on the arrival times. Zach was giving off nervous energy by pacing around and looking out of the window every few minutes. Maya had been over twice in between appointments to see if Ace had heard anything about the dogs' ETA.

When Ace heard the crunch of tires driving over the pebbled driveway, he felt butterflies flittering around in his stomach. One look out the window confirmed his hunch that the dogs had arrived. A white transport van was sitting outside. "Zach. The dogs are here," he called out. Within seconds, Zach made a beeline for the door, exiting the building in lockstep with Ace. When they opened the door, Maya was standing there with an anxious look etched on her face. She resembled a little kid on the first day of kindergarten.

"I don't know why I'm so nervous," Maya said, clenching and unclenching her hands. "I deal with animals every day. It feels like Christmas morning when I was a little kid. Bess and I were always up at the crack of dawn waiting to open our presents."

"Same here. It's like that funny feeling I get when I ride a roller coaster," Zach said, rubbing his hands together and peering over at the van.

"Nervous excitement," Ace said. "It just means we're all invested and we want everything to run smoothly."

Ace had been full of jitters for days. This morning he'd woken up and gotten down on his knees to pray for a successful launch. Most of all, he'd prayed that they could provide comfort and healing to these dogs and serve as a bridge to their forever families. It would be such a blessing if the townsfolk opened their homes and their hearts to the rescue dogs.

There were twelve dogs in all—one dalmatian, two huskies, two malamutes, two Labradors, one boxer, two pit bulls, one Chihuahua and one terrier mix. In Ace's opinion they were all wonderful and fascinating and amazing. For the first few hours Zach and Ace got the dogs acclimated to their new surroundings with Maya popping in between clients.

"I wish that I could stay over here all day," Maya said as she cradled a terrier in her arms during a quick visit with the rescue dogs. "But duty calls. I have an appointment with a very cantankerous Siamese cat." She placed the dog on the floor and scrambled to her feet.

"We've got it all under control," Ace said. "Don't we, Zach?"

"I don't think there's anything we haven't planned for," Zach said, grinning so widely Ace thought his face might break. He winked at Maya. "We've got this."

Ace wasn't sure if Zach was flirting with Maya, but the very idea of it annoyed him. *What was wrong with him?* He had no right to feel this way. Ace knew how goofy his younger brother could be, so this was par for the course for him. He was overreacting and it nagged at him. Why did it feel as if all of his emotions were riding on the surface these days?

"We'll take pictures when we can," Ace

said. "I've been thinking that creating a web-site for the rescue is a good idea, as well as setting up an Instagram page where we can post the dogs, their names and the cost of adoption. It will really increase our visibility, especially with the younger demographic," Ace explained.

"That's a great idea," Zach said. "That way if someone sees a dog they're interested in they can head on over, fill out the applica-tion, pay the fee and take home their dog of choice. Because we know everyone in town, preapproval for adoption will be considered for most applicants."

Maya let out an excited sound. "I love that idea. It's brilliant. Social media is everything these days." She made a face. "I really need to ramp up the website for the Best Friends clinic. Dad wasn't into the bells and whistles for the veterinary clinic, so it's pretty bare-bones."

"No time like the present," Ace said. "You can also put a link to the dog-rescue site. It'll be a win-win situation for both the clinic and the shelter."

"That's why you're the perfect person to lead the dog rescue," she said playfully, beaming up at him. "Well, I'll check in later with you guys." With a wave of her hand she was gone, taking a dose of sunshine with her. Ace couldn't really explain it in words, but he always felt a jolt of energy in the atmosphere when Maya was around.

As soon as she walked away, Ace felt Zach staring at him.

"You two seem like you're…on good terms," Zach said, emphasizing the word *good*.

Ace met Zach's gaze unflinchingly. "Yeah… and?" He knew Zach was insinuating something about him and Maya, but he wouldn't come right out and say it.

"I think it's great that the two of you can work together so well." He shrugged. "And if it leads to something more, that would be great, too."

"It won't," Ace said tersely. "We're just getting along for the greater good. It's all about the rescue dogs. Nothing more, nothing less."

"But who knows? It could be. That's the cool thing about life. We never know what's coming around the corner," Zach said, pressing the matter further than Ace felt he could deal with right now. He didn't need Zach spinning fairy tales.

"No, it won't be happening. I haven't forgotten the way she dumped me five years ago or the way she walked away, as if I'd meant nothing to her." He could hear the raw anger vibrating in his voice, but he couldn't rein it in. He needed to nip this talk in the bud or else Zach wouldn't let it go. "I'd be a fool to go down that road again after what she put me through. In case you're confused, I'm not an idiot. I have zero interest in dating Maya."

Zach's mouth hung open, and he was staring at something behind Ace.

When Ace turned around Maya was standing there, clearly having overheard their conversation, judging by her flushed cheeks and wide eyes.

"I—I just came back to get my jacket," she said, walking over to the chair and grabbing her white vet's coat. Without saying another word, she walked away, disappearing down the hall.

Zach let out a groan and covered his face with his hands.

"Just great," Ace muttered. It made him feel like a jerk knowing Maya had overheard his heated comments. Why did he keep putting his foot in his mouth? His words had been for Zach's ears only, but by some stroke of misfortune, Maya had gotten an earful.

"Maybe you should try and smooth things

over," Zach suggested. "That look on her face was pretty awful." Zach shuddered.

"What I said wasn't so bad," Ace said. He wasn't sure who he was trying to convince—himself or Zach.

"Surely you don't believe that. I've never even had a girlfriend, and I know better than that," Zach said, shaking his head as he walked toward the play area and began running around with the dogs.

Zach's comment kept nagging at him throughout the day, along with his memory of the crushed expression on Maya's face. Shouldn't he feel a teeny bit happy that he'd wounded her after the way she'd so cruelly dumped him?

But he didn't feel that way at all. It was strange to care so much about her feelings after all this time. And rather than dwell on it, Ace was going to focus one hundred percent on the rescue dogs and try his best to keep his emotions under wraps. He had a nagging feeling that it would be easier said than done.

Maya ran her forearm under the warm water and added some soap to clean her skin. She'd gotten scratched by her sassy feline patient, Fantasia, and it was important to clean the wound so it didn't get infected. Fantasia wasn't an awful cat by any means. The feline had a little bit of vet anxiety and had tried to wrangle her way out of Maya's arms. It wasn't the first time it had happened to Maya, but she was feeling a little sorry for herself. It wasn't hard for her to figure out the source of her irritable mood. It all led back to Ace and the conversation she'd overheard. There was no longer any point in wondering about his anger toward her. It all led straight back to her decision to break up with him.

She had to find a way to tell him the truth. Perhaps then he would understand why she'd made her decision. But things were complicated now that she'd been feeling ill again. Her appointment with Rachel was later this afternoon, so that would hopefully allay her fears about a leukemia recurrence. Maya didn't want to admit even to herself how scared she was about getting bad news. Battling cancer had been one of the toughest roads she'd ever traveled. Losing Bess had been the hardest, hands down. It was at moments like this that she wished Bess was still here so she could lean on her for strength and confide in her. She would continue to miss her sister for the rest of her days.

Maya didn't even have the heart to go check on the rescue dogs when she had a lull in her schedule. It felt best to stay away from Ace. He'd always been a hothead with a sharp tongue. But he'd also been as sweet as a box of North Star chocolates. No one had been as supportive as Ace when she'd been contemplating vet school. He'd even researched scholarships for her to apply for. It was getting harder and harder to forget everything they'd meant to one another.

After her last patient of the day, Maya headed over to the clinic where Rachel worked as a nurse. She resisted the temptation to check in at the shelter, with Ace's cutting words replaying in her mind. *The way she walked away, as if I'd meant nothing to her.* If only he knew, she thought. Breaking up with Ace had shattered her. The only reason she'd been able to wake up in the morning and function was out of a desire to beat the leukemia.

When she arrived at Rachel's clinic by the waterfront, Maya paused for a moment to admire the view. Even though it was April, patches of snow still covered the mountains looming in the distance. She inhaled deeply, allowing the pristine Alaskan air to fill her lungs. Her gaze trailed after two bald eagles who swooped down over the water to catch their prey.

Fishing boats were docked at the harbor as fishermen brought in their hauls for the day—crabs, salmon and halibut being the most common. She'd always loved looking out over the stunning waters of Kachemak Bay. When she was a little girl, her dad had taken her and Bess out on his sailboat so far out on the water it felt like they'd reached the ends of the earth. Ace had surprised her once with a sunset cruise along the harbor, complete with dinner, sparkling cider and candlelight. No wonder she'd fallen madly in love with him.

"Maya!" She turned toward the sound of her name being called. Rachel was standing in the doorway, waving at her. Maya walked toward her, then reached out and hugged her old friend. With her warm brown skin, dark wavy hair and classic features, Rachel was a stunning woman.

"It's been a while since I've seen you," Rachel said, leading her inside the building. Although it was small, the interior was very appealing, with a soothing color scheme, rustic decor and comfy furniture.

"I've been swamped at the vet clinic," Maya explained. "And we just opened our dog rescue today, so things are going to get even busier."

Rachel nodded as she waved Maya into an examination room. Maya sat down on the exam chair. "I know the feeling. I've been serving as a midwife in the community and there's been a baby boom." Her eyes twinkled. "Gabriel and I haven't announced it yet, but we're expecting our own bundle of joy in the fall."

"Oh, Rachel. That's wonderful news," Maya gushed. "Thanks for sharing it with me." Maya was happy for Rachel and Gabriel. Separated for many years due to fear and misunderstandings, they'd reunited last year and finally tied the knot. It was hard for Maya not to feel a tad bit envious. Rachel's life seemed full of the perfect balance between her vocation and personal life.

"Okay, let's get down to business," Rachel said, sitting down on a stool with an iPad in her hand. "What brings you here? I know you said on the phone that you hadn't been feeling well."

"I haven't. The other day I felt faint and nauseous…really out of it." She ran a hand through her hair. "And ever since then I haven't felt like my normal self."

"Any underlying conditions I need to know about?" Rachel asked.

Maya let out a sigh. "I had leukemia five years ago, but I beat it. And I've been healthy until now."

Rachel raised her eyebrows. "I had no idea, Maya. I was gone from Owl Creek for a while, but I haven't even heard a whisper that you were ill."

"That's because my treatment took place in Seattle, and the only person I told was Florence," Maya explained.

Rachel looked at her with disbelief. "Oh, wow. You didn't even tell your family? Or Ace?"

"No, they still have no idea." Just saying the words out loud caused a feeling of shame to sweep over her. She still wrestled with the choice she'd made.

"That's an awful burden to carry around on your shoulders. Trust me, I'm not judging you because I've harbored my own secrets, but stress might be the cause of your physical symptoms," Rachel said.

"True, but the scary part is these are the exact same symptoms I was experiencing before my initial diagnosis. It's really messing with my head." Maya let out a sob. The pressure of being in this situation was wreaking havoc on her. Just when her life was getting settled, she'd been brought to her knees by the possibility of being ill once again.

Rachel reached out and squeezed Maya's hand. "First of all, I want you to be careful about jumping to conclusions. You don't know anything at the moment. Fear of being sick again can be making things worse."

"It's been my biggest worry for a very long time that the leukemia would return," Maya confessed.

"I can tell you from my own personal experience that cancer can be beatable and treatable, which you clearly know from your own encounter with it. Even if your leukemia has returned, it's not a foregone conclusion that you won't make it. My mother battled breast cancer not too long ago, so I understand all too well the angst and worry. But don't let it overwhelm you."

Maya knew that what Rachel was telling her was accurate, but it didn't erase her anxiety. "I'd feel much better if you could run some tests." At least she would know if her life was once again at risk. Everyone always said God never gave you more than you could handle, but at the moment, she wasn't sure it was true.

"Of course, Maya. I'll do whatever it takes to give you peace. I'll take some blood samples and we'll get to the bottom of this," Rachel said with a bob of her head. "Now let's get a blood-pressure reading and a few other things done before I take your blood. I'll be consulting with Dr. Porter on your case and the sample will be tested for any abnormalities. He shares the space with me, and he's been in practice for almost twenty years. He'll be coming in shortly to meet with you. Once we get those results we can reach out to your oncologist in California so they can be kept in the loop."

Tears pooled in Maya's eyes, and she blinked them away. Rachel's bedside manner was soothing. She felt grateful to be receiving medical advice from a trusted friend rather than going to a stranger who might not have been so gentle. Although she was still nervous, Maya felt calmed by Rachel's reassurances and by the knowledge that tests would be run on her. She took a deep breath as her blood was drawn.

She prayed that she would have the strength

to endure whatever came her way. With her previous bout with cancer she'd wished Ace had been around for her to lean on. His quiet strength would have been a huge support. But, because of her decision to keep him in the dark, she'd dealt with it on her own in Seattle. Although Florence had flown in for a few chemo sessions, she hadn't been able to keep traveling back and forth from Alaska, which Maya had completely understood. But this time around, she had no intention of hiding anything. She wished she'd never gone down that road in the first place.

Lord, I need Your help. Hold me in the palm of Your hand and guide me through this dark moment. I'm not sure that I'm strong enough to go through this again.

One way or the other, Maya knew she would soon discover if her leukemia had returned.

Chapter Ten

Days passed without Ace seeing much of Maya. He couldn't help but feel that she was avoiding him due to the way he'd spoken to Zach about their breakup. His comment about not wanting to date Maya again had been hurtful. He hadn't known she was in earshot at the time, but given the fact that he was working at the dog rescue she'd created, it hadn't been cool at all.

It was time for him to swallow his pride and apologize. Why was it always so hard for him to say he was sorry? His mother used to call him bullheaded. He remembered Blue telling him that one day he would choke on his pride. Ever since the sled crash Ace had been trying to grow and change. Almost losing Luna and ending his racing career had been incredibly humbling. In an instant he'd been forced to realize what was truly important in the grand scheme of things.

He let out a groan. There was no time like the present to make things right.

Around lunchtime he headed into the clinic, seeking out Maya. The office staff took their lunch at noon so he figured there wouldn't be any clients inside. He'd seen Peggy heading out of the lot in her vehicle a little while ago with a coworker. When he walked inside the building, the waiting room was empty. He relaxed a little, knowing he wouldn't have an audience.

He walked down the hall, immediately noticing that Maya's door was wide open. She was sitting at her desk with her head down as she ate her lunch and gazed at her computer. Clearly, she hadn't heard his footsteps. He took a moment to simply appreciate the graceful slope of her neck and the look of intense concentration etched on her face. Ace knocked softly to get her attention, causing her to quickly look up from her computer.

Maya seemed taken aback at the sight of him. It made him sad remembering how she used to light up when he paid her a visit. He shouldn't expect things to be the same as they'd once been, but it hurt to know how much everything had changed. Ace missed being that special someone in her life, although he didn't want to examine his feelings too closely.

"I'm sorry to bother you, Maya, especially during your lunch break," Ace said, shifting from one foot to the other.

"No worries," she said, picking up a napkin and wiping her mouth. She pushed her salad to the side of her desk. "I was just finishing up. What's going on? Is everything running smoothly over at the shelter? I've been meaning to come over and check in, but things have been pretty hectic over here. I've done a lot of spaying and neutering in the past few days."

"Well, I'm just going to say it," he said sheepishly. "I was thinking maybe you were avoiding me."

She paused for a moment, then said, "I'll be honest. Overhearing your conversation with Zach wasn't pleasant." She wrinkled her nose. "But you have every right to feel that way. How can I be upset at something you were privately sharing with your brother?"

"So you're not staying away from the rescue because of me?" Ace asked, surprised by Maya's statement. She was letting him off the hook.

Maya stood up and came from behind her desk. "No, I promise you I'm not keeping away for that reason. It's just been a rough few days."

Ace saw something on her face that he didn't like. Despite the lost years between them, he could still read her extremely well. Something wasn't quite right. And that wasn't okay with him.

"Don't take this the wrong way, but you look a bit frazzled. Is everything okay?" he asked. Ace was genuinely concerned about her. Maybe that was part of the problem. He cared too much. Even though they were no longer together, it didn't mean he'd stopped caring, even though for so many years he'd told himself he didn't.

"I—I'm just a bit preoccupied about something," she admitted. "It's weighing heavily on my mind. I didn't sleep very well last night." There was a little hitch in her voice, and he saw a sheen of tears pooling in her eyes. Seeing her like this gutted him. He hated the idea of Maya being upset.

"I know I may not be the ideal person to talk to, but I'm here if you need someone to unload on. And I can keep a secret like no-body's business," he said. "You can trust me."

"That's really sweet of you, Ace. I know what a good man you are," she said, dabbing at her eyes with her fingers. "And I'm so sorry I hurt you. It was never my intention…" She stopped talking in midsentence, her lips trembling with emotion.

Ace walked toward her, quickly swallowing up the distance between them in seconds. He reached out and lifted up her chin, wanting desperately to comfort her. Their eyes locked and held. "You're one of the kindest people I've ever known," Ace said. He reached out and pushed her hair away from her face. "And in case no one has told you lately, you're beautiful, inside and out."

He lowered his head and tenderly placed his lips on hers. As soon as their mouths touched, Ace knew he was a goner. Maya's lips tasted like spun sugar, as if she'd just eaten something sweet. He placed his hands on either side of her face, anchoring her to him. She kissed him back with equal measure, reaching out to grab ahold of the collar of his shirt to pull him closer. As the kiss intensified, Ace found himself wishing he could suspend time to make it last for a long time instead of these fleeting moments.

He'd been thinking of doing this since the moment he'd brought Luna into her clinic. There was no longer any point in denying it. And it felt so incredibly right, as if their lips were meant to be joined. It wasn't like him to think in such romantic terms, but Maya had always brought out this side of him. She'd inspired him to be sweeter and gentler.

As the kiss ended, Maya whispered his name against his lips. He ran his hands through her hair, twirling it around his fingers before letting the strands go. The aroma of roses filled his nostrils—Maya's special scent. It always reminded him of this incredible woman.

The sound of a door closing alerted them to the fact that they were no longer alone. A few seconds earlier and they might have been interrupted by one of Maya's staff members or a client, Ace realized.

"Peggy must be back from lunch," Maya explained, darting a glance toward the corridor.

"I should get back to work," Ace said, stepping away from Maya. The last thing he wanted was for any gossip to spark about him and Maya being alone in her office when no one else was around. He knew all too well how quickly gossip could spread in a small town like Owl Creek. Maya had worked hard to build a professional reputation and he didn't want anything to jeopardize it, especially not whispers about the two of them.

"Okay. I'll stop by later to check in and we can talk about setting up a table at the Spring Fling," Maya said.

"Sounds good," he responded with a nod. At this point he couldn't get away fast enough. He was still a bit shocked that he'd actually kissed her.

As he walked back over to the shelter, Ace thought about the intimate moment he'd just shared with Maya. There was no denying their chemistry. It had felt like fireworks on the Fourth of July. Nothing had changed in that regard in all these years, but everything else between them had shifted.

Kissing her had been impulsive. His stomach was now in knots. It had been a huge mistake, one that he couldn't take back. *What had come over him?* Maya was no longer the love of his life. They had no romantic future. He still didn't have any answers about what had happened to cause her to dump him so abruptly. Sharing a romantic kiss with her hadn't changed a thing for them, other than further complicating a very muddled situation.

It could never happen again. It was that simple. And incredibly difficult at the same time. For five long years he'd packed away his feelings for the only woman he'd ever truly loved. Keeping his emotions bottled up inside hadn't erased them. And now, the scintillating kiss they'd just shared served to remind him of everything he'd been missing but couldn't have.

Maya fanned her flushed face several times during the course of the day as she remembered her kiss with Ace. She touched her lips with her fingertips. Her mouth still felt singed. He'd been tender and romantic, treating her the way he'd done during their courtship.

It was hard not to acknowledge she was battling old feelings that were now resurfacing. Her natural instinct was to tamp them down since she knew it would be impossible to forge anything new with Ace. How could she when the truth still stood between them? It wouldn't be fair to start something up again when she was possibly facing a serious health challenge. Not to mention she had overheard him telling Zach that being with her was out of the question. For him it could have simply been a spontaneous act and not tied to any feelings for her. Either way, Maya intended to put it in her rearview mirror. She had enough to contend with at the moment, in particular her health and the opening of the dog rescue.

When she was able to carve out a little time in her day to head over to the shelter, Maya walked in on an adoption in progress.

"Otis! What are you doing here?" Maya asked upon seeing her sweet friend cradling an adorable Chihuahua named Frenchy. She remembered seeing Frenchy's file and thinking she would make a wonderful companion. After being abandoned by her owner, Frenchy was in need of love and support.

Otis pointed at the lovely gray-haired woman standing next to him. "I came with my good friend Birdie. She wanted to come down here and check out the rescues. I don't think I'm exaggerating by saying it was love at first sight when she saw Frenchy."

Birdie McCuller laughed along with Otis, showcasing her dimples. "He's right, Doc Roberts. I'm head over heels."

Maya still hadn't gotten used to being called Doc Roberts by the townsfolk. It always automatically made her think of her father. But, now that he'd retired, Maya was going to have to get used to the title.

Ace walked up on their conversation and handed Birdie some paperwork. "It's official. You and Frenchy belong to each other." A nice, easy smile stretched out across Ace's face. Just seeing it caused butterflies to flitter around in Maya's stomach. It was fantastic seeing this side of him. It was the same sort of joy he'd radiated when he was racing his sled-dog team. She suspected that time was healing the emotional wounds surrounding the accident, while being in the presence of the rescue dogs was helping him to bounce back.

Birdie took Frenchy from Otis and placed a kiss on her temple. Tears glistened in her eyes. "I want to thank you from the bottom of my heart for making this lifelong dream come true." She sniffled. "I always wanted a dog, but for one reason or another it never came to pass. Jerry, bless his soul, was allergic," she explained, referencing her deceased husband. "I just can't wait to have a bunch of adventures with Frenchy."

Otis placed his arm around Birdie, and

they sailed out the door with huge grins on their faces. This, Maya thought, was the type of happy ending she'd envisioned for rescue dogs.

"Are they...a couple?" Maya asked, delighted at the notion that Otis had found love at this stage in his life.

"They are indeed," Ace said. "They bonded over pie-making. Those berry pies sure are made with love," he teased, his eyes full of mirth.

Maya shook her head and chuckled. "I'm happy for them. It just shows that it's never too late to find love. And they were friends first, so that's even sweeter."

Ace knit his eyebrows together and stared at her intensely. He opened his mouth to say something just as Zach walked over with a tall, ginger-haired young woman, whom he quickly introduced as Olivia Walker, one of their new volunteers. Sierra, Daisy's rescuer, had also become a volunteer.

"Welcome. We're very glad to have you on board," Maya said. It was a relief to know that there would be more hands on deck to help care for the dogs. Pretty soon, more dogs would be arriving and they'd reach full capacity even though they would never deny any dog their services.

"Thanks, Maya," Olivia said. "I'm really happy to be here helping out."

After exchanging pleasantries, Olivia headed over to the play area to occupy the dogs while Maya spoke with Ace and Zach about putting together some sort of demonstration for the town's Spring Fling event. Although they didn't have much time to pull something together, they all agreed that showcasing the dogs would be a crucial component of their adoption campaign.

"Why don't we bring along a few of the dogs so the townsfolk can check them out," Ace suggested. "They can play with them and see how bright and lively they are. We'll give them a chance to fall in love with them like Birdie did."

"That sounds wonderful," Maya said. "We'll be giving them hands-on experiences with the dogs. There's nothing quite like it—seeing, touching, smelling. Speaking of which, we should make sure they're all bathed and smelling nice and fresh."

"Will do," Ace said.

"I can make up a flier with information about the costs of adopting as well as our contact number and some stats on rescues," Zach added.

"I like that," Maya said, her excitement growing by the minute. "I'm constantly being asked about adoption fees for rescues. Folks just don't understand the costs associated with running a rescue or medical costs."

"We'll educate them on it so they understand what goes on behind the scenes," Ace said. "From what I remember, that event is always packed with people. It'll be a great opportunity to get the word out."

The Spring Fling festival was Maya's favorite town event. There was food and music and socializing. Although she loved winter in Owl Creek, this celebration heralded the arrival of warmer temperatures and the birth of moose calves and the end of bear hibernation. Whales and other marine animals returned to Kachemak Bay. As a veterinarian, she loved to witness an increase in wildlife activity.

She caught Ace staring at her a few times, and she wondered if he was thinking about the kiss they'd shared. Thankfully, Zach was there to serve as a buffer. She wasn't sure that she could handle any more alone time with Ace today. As it was, he was never far away from her thoughts and it was beginning to worry her. Ace had been a huge part of her world for many years, but she'd firmly placed him in the past after their breakup. But now, with him being in such close proximity to the clinic, he was once again a part of her day-to-day life. It was impossible to ignore his solid, rugged presence.

Maya knew it would be a long time before she stopped thinking about the mesmerizing kiss they'd shared, and wondered if there would be others in their future.

Chapter Eleven

The morning of the Spring Fling festival dawned bright and beautiful. The sun was shining in a clear blue sky the color of a robin's egg. Last night there had been a short burst of snow flurries, but the snow had barely stuck to the ground. As a born-and-bred Alaskan, Ace had seen his fair share of snowstorms in April. He was thankful they hadn't gotten hit with another one.

Ace was outside playing with his dogs, throwing tennis balls and Frisbees around the fenced-in area. He'd been so busy at work lately that he hadn't had ample time to spend with these dogs of his heart. Blue, on the other hand, was spending plenty of quality time with them and doing a phenomenal job of caring for them.

"Come on, Chai. Give me the Frisbee," Ace

called out after Chai caught it in midair and came trotting back to him. Zach was outside with them but he was on his cell phone talking to a young lady he was trying to impress. Listening to his flowery language made Ace chuckle. It reminded him of himself at Zach's age, always trying to woo one girl after another. Until he met Maya. He'd been so smitten he'd never looked at another girl again.

"Are you going, too, Dad?" Ace asked, watching as his father tended to his dogs. He'd noticed that ever since Blue had been spending his days with Ace's dogs, he seemed more upbeat and outgoing. Perhaps it was the fact that he no longer had the overdue mortgage balance hanging over his head, but he seemed as if he was enjoying life more. Ace hadn't seen him like this since before his mother passed away.

"I wouldn't miss it for the world," Blue said. "I love your dogs, Ace, but going to the festival will give me a little break from them." He rubbed his hands together. "I've been looking forward to some reindeer pizza and crab chowder."

"Mmm. Sounds good to me," Ace said. Alaskan food was the best. He was excited to attend the festival for numerous reasons.

Mainly, it was the perfect way to introduce the dogs to Owl Creek and get some attention for the center. He was in a better place, now that he'd dealt with the fallout from his sled crash. Ace was no longer reluctant to face the residents of his hometown. He no longer walked around with his huge albatross hanging around his neck. Both Otis and Maya had helped him to realize that.

One of the highlights of the event was the fare from the local restaurants, as his father had indicated. There was also music, usually a local indie band performing. What he'd always enjoyed the most was the camaraderie. Would he still fit in with the locals? It had been a long time since he'd hung out with them. For so long he'd let pride get in the way of bolstering those connections.

By the time he and Zach arrived at the fairgrounds, Maya was already there, accompanied by her own two dogs, Betty and Veronica. She was setting up a table and struggling to get the table legs to behave. Ace put his truck in Park and raced over to help her out.

"I've got it," Ace said as he took the table off her hands and flipped it on its side so he could work on the legs. With a few manipulations on his part, the table was in working order. He flipped it back around and placed it back down on the ground.

"Thanks," Maya said, huffing out a breath. She looked a little tired, he realized. He hoped she wasn't still tossing and turning at night with worry. She still looked beautiful, dressed in a red barn jacket and formfitting, dark-washed jeans. Her hair hung softly in waves around her face and she wasn't wearing a stitch of makeup other than something shiny on her lips.

Ace and Zach had stopped by the rescue to pick up four of the dogs to feature at the event. Olivia and River, another volunteer, had agreed to hold down the fort at the rescue while they were gone. Ace turned back toward his truck to help Zach with getting the dogs unloaded. They'd brought along Zorro, a dalmatian, a terrier named Falcon, a boxer named Poppy, and Marley, a malamute.

They put up a cardboard sign and decorated the table with photos of the dogs Ace had printed out. Zach placed his flyers front and center, where they could easily be seen. Maya tied balloons on either end of the table, lending it a festive look. It was a great day to show off the rescue dogs. Now they just had to sit back and watch as the canines melted the hearts of all the Owl Creek residents.

It was turning out to be a great event, Maya thought as she looked around the fairgrounds. Townsfolk had shown up in droves to celebrate the spring season. Her vet clinic was closed this morning, with all emergency calls being forwarded to her cell phone. Maya could easily leave things in Ace's and Zach's hands if she was called away.

Just watching the interaction between Ace and Zach made Maya happy. They'd grown closer in the last few weeks and Zach had shown that he was dependable and dedicated. His love for dogs rivaled Ace's. It was gratifying to see them come full circle.

She felt tired today. Unusually fatigued. She'd been tempted to reach out to Rachel for her test results, but she knew her friend well enough to know she would call as soon as the results came in. It was so hard to wait on pins and needles for a medical diagnosis. Her very life hung in the balance.

Thankfully, she'd thought to bring a chair so she could sit down at different intervals when she felt completely wiped out. A few times she caught Ace gazing at her with a furrowed brow, as if he was confused, but she didn't think he suspected she might be ill. Maya prayed she never had to deliver such news to him or to anyone else she cared about. Working together on this dog-rescue project had been tension-filled at times, but it had also brought her and Ace closer together. She felt blessed to have Ace in her life again. The fact that he was playing such a large role in her dream project was serendipitous.

"It's a perfect day to adopt a rescue dog," Maya said in her most cheerful voice to Sage North and her toddler daughter as they walked up. "Hey there, Sage. I imagine Addie would love a dog." Sage, Beulah's granddaughter, was a local teacher married to Sheriff Hank Crawford, Piper's brother.

"They're all awfully cute. Especially this one," Sage said, reaching down and patting the terrier.

"That's Falcon," Ace said, looking on like a proud papa. "He's very gentle and playful. He's one of those dogs who loves everyone."

"Doggy," Addie said, reaching out and tightly hugging Falcon.

"Why don't we see what Daddy says?" Sage asked, gently pulling Addie away. She made a face and whispered, "I think if she had a choice we'd be taking Falcon home right now."

"I can see that," Maya said with a laugh. "Talk to Hank. It's a big decision for your family." Although Maya wanted all of the rescues in her care to find forever homes, it had to be right for the family and the dog. It was always sad when things didn't work out and a rescue dog was returned to the shelter.

"I'll take a flyer so I have all of the information," Sage said, picking one up from the table. Maya appreciated her pragmatism and how seriously she was considering dog adoption.

When Sage walked away holding Addie's hand, Ace said with a grin, "I think she's definitely coming back for Falcon."

"I don't know," Maya said, biting her lip. "It could go either way, but I'm really pulling for Falcon to join their family."

"Let's dream big today," Ace said. "It's very possible that it'll work out. Who knows? All of these dogs might be adopted."

"Hey, guys," Zach said. "Do you mind if I take a little break? I want to check out one of the bands."

"One of the bands, huh? Not the girl you were on the phone with earlier?" Ace asked, smirking at Zach, whose face blushed with embarrassment.

"Go ahead. It's fine, Zach," Maya said, shaking her head at Ace. As soon as Zach disappeared, Maya added, "Leave him alone. He's been working so hard these last few weeks. He deserves to have some fun."

"I was just teasing. I have to admit, I'm mighty proud of him. He's really evolving. You were right, Maya, about giving him a shot."

Just then, Ace's grandparents walked up along with his dad, Blue. Just the sight of his family members made her feel emotional. Once, they had been such a big part of her world. They'd always been loving and supportive and kind to her. All of them had been shocked when she and Ace had parted ways. They'd all been under the belief that a wedding was around the corner. She'd never known what to say to make them understand, so she hadn't really tried.

"Maya!" they called out, rushing over to embrace her.

Ace's grandparents, Walter and Geraldine, had been childhood sweethearts. Now married for sixty-two years, they were still as in love as ever. Maya enjoyed seeing them in town—they were always holding hands and supporting one another.

"You're such a welcome sight," Geraldine crowed as she looked Maya up and down, her gaze filled with admiration.

"If it isn't the prettiest girl in Owl Creek," Walter said with a huge grin. "And the smartest, too. Maybe we should be calling you Dr. Roberts."

"You're going to give me a swollen head," Maya teased.

"Don't tell Ace, but I always say you're the one who got away." His grandfather's eyes twinkled mischievously.

"Ace is right here, and he can hear you," Ace said, rolling his eyes.

His grandfather let out a huge belly laugh. "We're not trying to hide anything. We believe in full transparency."

Blue began chuckling along with them. Maya had to work hard not to crack a smile.

"Leave the boy alone, Walter," Geraldine chided him. "You're embarrassing him."

Walter waved off her comment. "Ace is a big boy, Geraldine. He can handle a little ribbing from his grandpa."

"Don't worry, Gran," Ace said with a wink. "I've got tough skin."

"How are the dog adoptions going?" Blue asked, swiftly changing the subject. "Anyone biting?"

"A few interested parties, but no applications so far," Maya said, wishing she had better news to report.

"It's still early," Ace said, sounding more hopeful than she felt. It was a little bit of a heartbreak to think they might not have anyone interested in dog adoptions today. Maya needed to be patient and keep the faith.

"We hope all of your dogs are scooped up," Geraldine said, clapping her hands together. "We'll be praying for it."

"We're heading out," Walter said, placing his arm around his wife. "Geraldine is feeling a bit tuckered out."

"And I have an awful headache," she said, wincing and raising her fingers to her forehead.

"I'm dropping them home," Blue said. "I'll see you folks later. Make sure Zach gets a ride back home."

"Feel better, Gran," Ace said as he dipped his head down to press a kiss on her cheek.

"If they're not the sweetest," Maya said, her gaze trailing after them as they headed to the lot. "I want to be like Geraldine and Walter when I grow up."

A wistful expression was etched on Ace's face. "You're not the only one."

For a moment, Maya found herself wondering if she and Ace would have wound up like his grandparents if she hadn't abruptly ended things, thereby altering the course of their relationship. It was a sobering thought. She wouldn't ever truly know if her act of sacrifice had been worth it. And although she'd thought about telling Ace the truth, her current health situation muddied the waters. If she was sick again, Maya would be back at square one. But if she wasn't…coming clean with Ace might lead to closure between them. Wasn't that what she owed him? Some sort of explanation for torpedoing their romance?

Just then Sage walked back over with Hank, who was holding Addie in his arms. Hank let his daughter down and she toddled over toward the dogs.

"Doggy," she said, pointing toward Falcon, who ran straight over toward her with his tail wagging. "My doggy," she said, patting him on the head. She was rewarded with an enthusiastic lick. Maya didn't think it could get any more adorable than this moment.

"We're making it official," Hank said. "We're adopting Falcon. Addie can't stop talking about bringing him home with us."

Maya and Ace let up a celebratory cheer and cries of excitement. As they handed Sage and Hank documents to fill out, Addie continued to get acquainted with her new dog as Maya looked on. It was Maya's pleasure to inform them that they'd been preapproved for adoption since she knew their family so well. Falcon was such a gentle pup and Maya felt very confident that this adoption was going to work out. Poor Falcon had been through a lot in his young life, and this was a huge step toward his happily-ever-after.

After handing over a bag filled with an extra collar, a small bag of dog food and some toys, Maya and Ace stood and watched Falcon trot off with his new family.

Maya could feel a huge smile stretching out across her face. "This makes me deliriously happy," Maya said, looking over at Ace. "Our very first dog adoption through the Owl Creek Dog Rescue."

"Happiness looks good on you," Ace said, his eyes lingering a little too long on her. Their gazes held, and in that moment, it seemed as if all was right between them. Ever since their kiss, Maya had been wondering if it was possible that she and Ace were slowy finding their way back to each other. Was it at all possible? She didn't think they could forge anything new unless she came clean with him about the past.

For the remainder of the afternoon they worked as a team, pitching the dogs and the other rescues to the townsfolk. Late in the day, Maya's parents stopped by their table.

After hugs and pleasantries were exchanged with Ace and Zach, her mom made an announcement. "We've decided to get a dog now that your dad is retired," Gigi said, looping her arm through her husband's. "Isn't that right, Vance?"

"I didn't think I'd ever get another dog after Jax passed away, but your mother convinced me," her dad said, looking down adoringly at his wife. Jax was their family dog, a German shepherd who had lived to fourteen years old. For Maya, Jax had set the standard for dogs in her life. Loyal and loving to a fault, Jax had been everything to the Roberts family.

Maya wagged her finger at her parents. "Why didn't you tell me you were thinking about getting a dog?" she asked, feeling completely shocked by this turn of events. Because her parents had never fully gotten over the loss of Jax, she'd never even bugged them about taking in one of her rescue dogs.

"There are so few surprises in life, we figured this one would make you smile." Vance reached out and squeezed his daughter's hand. "You have a world-class smile. Doesn't she, Ace?"

For a second Ace resembled a deer caught in the headlights. Maya wanted to sink into the ground with embarrassment due to her father putting him on the spot like this. A few seconds later Ace nodded and said, "She sure does. Second to none."

Just hearing Ace respond that way caused her pulse to quicken. It was sweet of him to compliment her, but she wasn't sure if he meant it or was simply pacifying her father. Maya had no idea what her father was playing at since he was well aware of her and Ace's tangled history. She wondered if this was his not-so-subtle way of trying to test the waters between her and Ace.

"I'd be happy to show you the dogs we brought along today," Ace offered. Her parents readily agreed and spent half an hour hanging out with the three rescue dogs. It wasn't long before they'd made a decision. Poppy, the boxer, was going home with them.

When Poppy was officially adopted by her parents, Maya almost broke down and cried. The boxer's history was filled with tragedy and resilience. Left for dead after being shot, Poppy had survived and thrived after two surgeries to save her life. It was a triumphant moment seeing Poppy end up with her very own parents. Maya honestly didn't think she could be any happier.

"Are you crying?" Zach asked, gaping at her. He took two steps away from her.

"N-no," she said. "I think there might be something in my eye." She began blinking furiously, trying to stem the tears.

Zach and Ace looked at each other and said in unison, "You're crying."

"Oh, come on," Maya said. "Don't tell me you didn't feel something tugging at your heartstrings. It's been so joyful to see good things happening for our rescue dogs."

"You're right about that, Maya," Ace said. "Just knowing that Falcon and Poppy have forever families is a blessing. Hopefully, we'll see this happen over and over again until the shelter is empty."

"From your lips to God's ears," Maya murmured. Most shelters were never completely cleared of canines, but it was something wonderful to hope for. In the Owl Creek community, anything was possible. Big hearts and generosity were in abundance.

Ace's phone buzzed and he reached for his cell phone, quickly taking the call as he stepped a few paces away from her and Zach. Maya couldn't help but notice his body tensing up and the stunned expression that came over his face. When he ended the call, Maya could clearly see he'd received bad news.

"We've got to go, Zach. It's Gran. She suffered a bad fall at home and they think she might've hit her head. She's unconscious," Ace said in a strangled voice. "She's at Doc Porter's clinic."

Zach let out a distressed sound and began packing up his flyers and signs.

"Maya, can you take Zorro and Marley back to the shelter?" Ace asked, his voice sounding frantic with worry.

"Don't worry. I've got all of this. Just go and be with your family," Maya instructed. She didn't want either of them to waste a second when there was a family crisis brewing.

"Thank you. I'll keep you posted," Ace said, running toward his truck with Zach following closely at his heels. Seconds later, Ace roared off.

In an instant, a beautiful day had turned into a serious emergency. Maya wrapped her arms around her middle and stared at the truck as it barreled down the road. Tomorrow wasn't promised. Nor was happiness. It was something she kept getting reminded about over and over again. Maya pressed her eyes closed and prayed for Geraldine, as well as Ace's entire family. As soon as she gathered everything up and dropped off the dogs at the shelter and her own dogs with her parents, Maya intended to meet up with Ace at the medical clinic. She wanted to support him through this crisis in any way she could. That's what a person did when they cared about someone.

Right now, her emotions were crashing over her with the force of storm winds. She knew Ace well enough to know that he was reliving those awful moments when his mother succumbed to cancer. He would try to hide his fear, but it would be eating away at him. No matter what issues stood between them, Maya wanted to be by his side offering support.

As surprising as it was to acknowledge

it, Maya could no longer deny that Ace was still firmly lodged in her heart, even though she knew they could never be together. Maya couldn't run the risk of hurting Ace if her leukemia had returned. It would be too cruel to put him through an illness that she might not survive.

Chapter Twelve

Ace maneuvered the back roads like a pro as he raced to the medical clinic. He'd never driven this fast in his life. Fear grabbed him by the throat, propelling him to move in fast motion.

Based on his father's comments, he knew the situation was life-or-death. His sweet gran was in trouble. Zach sat next to him in the passenger seat, clenching and unclenching his hands.

"Is she going to be okay, Ace?" Zach asked, dread emanating from his voice.

"I don't know, Zach," Ace said. He needed to be honest with his brother so he wasn't caught off guard if their grandmother didn't make it. It wouldn't be fair to give him false hope. "I wish that I could promise you she'll be fine, but we both know it doesn't work like that." Losing their mother to a fast-spreading cancer had been brutal. It had shown them that life was unpredictable and you could be forced to say goodbye to someone in a heartbeat.

For the rest of the ride Zach was quiet. Ace wished he could do or say something to make him feel better. "Just pray," Ace said, darting a quick glance in his brother's direction. "That's the one thing we can do for Gran."

When they arrived at the clinic, Rachel greeted them at the door, ushering them into a private waiting room, where Blue and Walter were seated.

"How is she doing?" Ace asked, his heart dropping at the shattered expression on his grandfather's face. His heart was hammering a wild rhythm in his chest as he braced for bad news.

"She's with the doctor now," Rachel said, "and he's trying to stabilize her. She lost consciousness for a period of time, so we have to make sure she didn't suffer any permanent damage."

"Like brain damage?" Zach asked with wide eyes.

"Let's not get ahead of ourselves," Rachel said, patting his shoulder. "I'm going to check in with Doc Porter and then I'll circle back with an update. I know it's hard, but try to stay calm. Geraldine is a strong woman."

"Thanks, Rachel," Blue said. "We'll be waiting here for any word on her condition." He crossed his hands prayerfully in front of him.

After a half hour of waiting and pacing, Ace felt as if he was going out of his mind with worry. He knew from being at the clinic that there was a small room a few doors down reserved for prayers. "I'll be back in a few minutes. I'm heading toward the prayer room," he said, making a fast exit to the door. He had so much resting on his heart that needed to be expressed. At the moment, he wasn't any good to his family in his chaotic state. He needed to offer up some prayers in private and then he'd rejoin them.

Moments later Ace found himself in the soothing prayer room, which was decorated in hues of blue and cream. Serene paintings hung on the wall. An essential oil diffuser allowed a lavender scent to waft around the room. Despite the calm of his surroundings, a hundred different thoughts raced around in his head. All he kept thinking was that his grandmother was slipping away from him just

like his mother had. Pain roared through him.
His losses were piling up on top of one an-
other and it was hitting him hard. His moth-
er's death. Losing Maya. The dogsled crash,
Luna's amputation and the loss of his career.
Now Gran's accident. His head was spinning.

He heard the door opening behind him.
When he turned around Maya was standing
in the doorway looking as if she didn't know
whether to stay or leave.

"Maya! I didn't expect to see you here."

"I wanted to come to offer my support. I
didn't mean to disturb you. Your family updated me and told me where to find you."

"I appreciate it. I just needed a quiet place
to be," Ace admitted.

"If you want me to leave, I can go to the
other room," Maya said, taking a step backward.

"No. Please don't leave," he said, breathing
a sigh of relief as she stepped into the room
and closed the door behind her. "I came in
here to pray, but I can't find the words, Maya.
All I know is that I don't want to lose her. I've
already lost so much in my life. I know that
sounds selfish, but it's how I feel. I want to
scream out to God that He can't have her yet."

Maya walked toward him so that there

were only mere inches between them. "It isn't selfish to want your grandmother to live. You love her. And your family needs her to stick around, especially your grandfather," Maya said. "How is everyone holding up?"

"Zach's a wreck, although I'm not much better myself. I think being here reminds us of when we lost our mother. He was barely a teenager back then and not equipped to deal with such a staggering loss."

"I'm not sure we're ever ready for that, at any age," Maya said. "I was a teenager when Bess passed away, but even if I'd been much older the loss would have still brought me to my knees."

Ace's shoulders sagged. "He pushed through it the best way he could, but I feel like I let him down. I should have been there for him and done more to provide support through those agonizing days."

He felt Maya's hand on his back. "You were there for him, Ace. Your whole family was grieving and trying to process the loss. Everyone was hurting. Don't be so hard on yourself."

"And look at me now. I've burrowed myself away to deal with this situation rather than lift my family up and offer support. They need me and look where I am." He groaned. Why was it always his instinct to lick his wounds in private? He'd done the same thing when his relationship with Maya crashed and burned, and after the Iditarod crash. At some point he'd come to realize that it didn't lessen the pain any.

Tears stung his eyes. He didn't want to break down in front of Maya, but his emotions were threatening to spill over. Ace had always prided himself on being strong and that didn't include tears. It was the way his father had brought him up—never let them see you cry. But it hadn't served him very well in his life. He was tired of always being the tough guy who hid all his hurts away.

He closed his eyes and began praying out loud. "God, if You're listening, we need some help that only You can provide. It's hard for me to ask for Gran's life to be spared, because I offered up those same prayers for my mother and they didn't work. Please help Gran. Give her the strength to pull through this." Overcome by emotion, he cleared his throat.

It was a big step for him to pray like this in the presence of another person. It felt like he was wearing his heart on the outside of his body. The notion that his prayer might not be answered frustrated him, but he knew God was listening.

"I'm here for you, Ace. Whatever you need." She tightly squeezed his hand.

Suddenly, Ace spotted a glint of gold on her wrist. He reached out and lifted the hem of her shirt so he could get a better view. "You kept it," he said, gently fingering the bracelet.

The wristlet had been a gift from Ace on their third anniversary. It was a one-of-a-kind piece of jewelry that he'd had commissioned from a jeweler in Anchorage. It had both of their initials engraved on it. Maya had loved it and worn it faithfully each and every day. He'd never imagined that she would continue to wear it all these years later.

Maya seemed a bit taken aback by him noticing the piece of jewelry. It probably wasn't something she wore every day, but maybe she put it on every now and again. She looked down at the bracelet, a soft smile gracing her beautiful face. "I loved it then and I love it now. It was the best gift anyone's ever given me. I remember that day so vividly. We were out in the woods with Luna, and you handed me this wooden box with a yellow bow on it. When you gave me the bracelet you told me it would last me my whole life." She swung her gaze up to meet his. "I couldn't bear to keep it in my jewelry box. It deserves to be worn."

Ace continued to finger the bracelet for a few beats, swinging his gaze up to look at her. They were standing so close together their bodies were almost touching. He could hear the sound of her light breathing. She was mere inches away from him. All he wanted to do in this moment was take her in his arms and kiss her. As impulsive as it might seem, it would be a life-affirming gesture. Ace felt like he was drowning. Maya could be his life preserver. He edged closer and closer.

Suddenly the door swung open with a bang. Blue was standing on the threshold, grinning from ear to ear. "Gran is awake, son," he said in an enthused voice. "And Rachel said her vitals look good, other than low blood sugar, which they're addressing as we speak. But the good news is that she's going to make it."

Ace's shoulders sagged in relief. He turned toward Maya, who was beaming up at him. Instinctively, he pulled her against his chest in a tight hug. A floral smell filled his nostrils, and he found himself wanting this embrace to last forever. She felt so right nestled in his arms. He was exactly where he wanted to be. And it scared him senseless.

The triumphant news about Geraldine hummed and pulsed in the air around them as the Reynoldses celebrated finding out that their matriarch was going to be just fine. Although she couldn't shout it from the rooftops, Maya was silently rejoicing over her own health update.

On the drive over to the clinic, Maya had listened to her voice-mail messages. Rachel had called to tell her that the test results had revealed severe anemia and there was no evidence of a leukemia recurrence. She wanted Maya to make an appointment at her earliest convenience so they could set up a treatment plan for her anemia. Maya had been incredibly relieved and thankful.

Between Rachel's upbeat message and Geraldine's recovery, Maya was feeling incredibly blessed.

Maya didn't know whether to stay or leave the clinic. It was amazing to be with Ace's family as they celebrated the news about Geraldine. She was incredibly happy for them, but she didn't want to overstep by intruding on their privacy. Just being with the Reynoldses made Maya realize how deeply she'd missed them over the years. She'd gone from being "one of the family" to a virtual stranger due to the breakup and her move to Seattle. And because of the secret she'd been keeping, there hadn't been an opportunity to explain her actions to Ace's loved ones. Regret seemed to be her constant companion these days.

Would she ever be at peace with the decision she'd made?

Rachel allowed all of them to come into Geraldine's private recovery room. When Maya stood back to allow Ace's family to go without her, Blue grabbed her by the hand and pulled her along with him. Although the older woman's face was a bit washed out, Maya thought she looked incredibly well, considering her ordeal.

Geraldine immediately waved off their concerns. "All this fuss over nothing," Geraldine said with a grimace. "I tripped on the walkway and bumped my head. I'd forgotten to eat anything due to all my excitement over the festival, which is why my blood sugar was low. I'm right as rain." She made a tutting sound.

"You gave us a good scare, Gran," Zach said, leaning in for a hug.

"I'm sorry about that," Geraldine said with a chuckle, "but you know I'm a troublemaker."

"Ain't it the truth," Ace teased. It was wonderful to see a relaxed expression on his face now that his gran was out of danger. She'd always loved his wonderful rapport with Geraldine. It was obvious she had a huge soft spot for Ace.

"They don't need to hold me overnight," Geraldine said as she tried to sit up in her bed.

Ace gently positioned her so she wasn't upright. "Just lay back until they tell you otherwise," he suggested. Although it earned him a frown from his grandmother, she didn't try to sit up again.

Walter patted her hand. "You need to follow doctor's orders, sweetie, so you can continue to get great reports from the doctor. I need you home with me, where you belong."

Geraldine tightly gripped her husband's hand. "In sixty-two years of marriage we've never spent a single night apart."

"That's true, my love. Maybe they'll let me stay over so we don't have to break our streak," Walter said with a wink.

Geraldine flashed him a beautiful smile. "Oh, Walter. Wouldn't that be wonderful?"

Maya thought her heart might crack into a million pieces. She was bearing witness to a love story for the ages. She'd always wanted a love like the one they shared. Once upon a time Maya thought she'd found it with Ace. It bothered her to think she'd thrown away her very own happily-ever-after.

"I think I'm going to head out," she said in a low voice to Ace. "I still have to pick up my dogs at my parents' house." She'd dropped off Betty and Veronica with them prior to coming over to the clinic. She said her goodbyes to Ace's family and placed a kiss on Geraldine's cheek.

"Thank you for coming to check in on me," Geraldine said. "It means the world to this old lady."

"It was my pleasure. Try to rest up," Maya said as she turned toward the door to leave.

"Let me walk you out," Ace suggested, coming up behind her and pulling open the door.

As they headed outside, Ace turned to her and said, "I can't thank you enough for coming by and being with us. It's been nerve-racking, but your being here helped more than you'll ever know."

"Your family means a lot to me. They always will," Maya admitted. For so many years they'd been her second family. She couldn't stop caring about them even if she tried.

Ace didn't say anything, but his surprised expression told his truth. Had he thought she'd simply stopped cherishing them? If so, perhaps that was her fault. It made her feel ashamed, although at the time she'd known any contact with Ace would have tempted her to run back into his arms and reunite with him.

Maya let out a gasp as the sky suddenly lit up in flashes of purple, green and silver. A bolt of pink undulated across the heavens. She couldn't remember ever seeing the northern lights in such a brilliant display of colors.

"I can't believe it," Ace said. "It's really late in the season to see the northern lights."

"Neither can I," she said with a laugh. "I guess we happened to be in the right place at the right moment."

"That's for sure. Most people have no idea what they're missing out on by not witnessing this," Ace said. "I don't think I'll see anything half as spectacular as the aurora borealis in my entire life."

She and Ace stood side by side, looking up toward the heavens as a spectacular light show unveiled itself to them. Neither of them said a word as it was going on, both content to feast their eyes on the shimmering spectacle. When it ended, Maya resisted the urge to start clapping. It felt as if she'd just witnessed an incredible production courtesy of Mother Nature.

"The only word that comes to mind is magnificent," she said, feeling grateful to be in Alaska at this very moment. Although she'd loved living in California, she couldn't experience anything quite like this in the Golden State.

"This is so strange. A few short hours ago I thought Gran was slipping away from us. And then the day ends with this incredible sight," Ace said, his voice sounding awestruck.

"Life pulls us in so many different directions," Maya said. "It really is true that things can change in a heartbeat. We can't take anything for granted along the way." Maya ducked her head. "That's why I'm taking this moment to tell you how much I value you. What you've done for the dog-rescue project is incredible. I wouldn't have been able to open its doors without you."

"That means a lot to me, Maya. At the same time, I need to tell you something. When you offered me the position I really was at a crossroads. Leaving dog racing behind left me in a real quandary about what to do next. Taking the lead position brought me back from a really low period in my life. So thank you for believing I could do it."

Maya looked up at him, resisting the urge to reach out and run her hand along his jawline.

"I've always believed you could do anything you set your mind to, Ace." It was true. Ace had always achieved excellence in all endeavors. Before his Iditarod crash, he'd racked up more wins than any racer in Alaskan dog-sledding history.

"Maya," Ace said in a low voice. He was looking at her with such a tender expression etched on his face. It reminded her of how it had once been between them. Some kind of wonderful. At the same time it hurt knowing they still had so much standing between them. Even if she told Ace the truth, she wasn't sure if he would accept what she'd done. She had no idea if it was possible to bridge the gap between them. But in this moment, she realized being with him was what she wanted more than anything in this world.

He reached out and held her chin between his fingers, looking deeply into her eyes. "Maya, I'm going to kiss you. If I'm being honest, I haven't been able to stop thinking about kissing you again since the other day." All Maya could do was nod. She wanted Ace to kiss her. Maybe this was nothing more than a dead end, but if so, she was still going to travel down this road with him. She swallowed past the fear. Why did it feel as if this was so much bigger than a kiss? It seemed more like a declaration between them. Of what, she wasn't completely sure.

He dipped his head and smoothly pressed his lips to hers. Maya responded without hesitation, placing her hands on his shoulders as the kiss intensified. It was full of tenderness and emotion. She felt Ace's hands around her waist pulling her closer. This kiss felt different from the previous kiss they'd shared at her office. That one had been spontaneous. This kiss felt right, as if they'd both intended to take this leap of faith together. This kiss meant something.

And she wouldn't mind if it lasted forever, this wonderful, soul-stirring kiss.

When they drew apart, Maya noticed that Ace's breathing was slightly labored. She imagined hers was as well, due to the exhilaration she felt. Today had been full of ups and downs, with a few surprises thrown in for good measure.

"I'm not sorry about kissing you, Maya," Ace said. "I know things between us ended a long time ago, but I can't help feeling as if we might not be done with each other."

"You're not the only one feeling that way," Maya said, running her palm along the side of his face. She couldn't help wanting to touch him…to connect with him after so many years of not having him in her life.

Ace grinned at her. "I'm relieved to hear that. I wasn't sure if I was imagining things."

"So what's next?" she asked, feeling a bit emboldened. Now that she knew that the leukemia hadn't come back, she felt much better about where things stood between them. She only had one more hurdle to jump over. Granted, it was a big one, but she couldn't continue to withhold the truth from Ace.

Ace quirked his mouth. "I don't want to complicate things for either of us, considering we have a professional relationship, but at the same time I don't want to walk away from something so powerful as what we have, either." Ace traced the outline of her lips with his finger.

"I walked away once before," she said with a shake of her head. "I can't do that again, Ace. I want to see where this goes, but there are things we need to discuss."

"Me, too, although I do think we need to talk about what went wrong last time." He ran a hand over his face. He seemed a bit weary. "I still have a lot of questions about why things went south between us. It's always been a bit of a mystery to me."

Maya's stomach twisted. She had so much to explain to Ace, but now wasn't the time. He really needed to get back inside the clinic so he could be with his family. And she needed to figure out how she was going to tell Ace and her parents about her battle with leukemia.

"Definitely," she said with a nod. "Before we consider moving toward the future we have to take a look at the past."

"I should go back inside," he said. "'Night, Maya." He leaned down and kissed her forehead. It made her feel hopeful. This night had been like no other, with the promise of reconciliation hovering in the air.

God's timing was never wrong.

"Good night, Ace," she said, admiring his tall, rugged frame as he walked away from her. As she got in her truck and began the drive back to her parents' house, her mind was racing at the prospect of finally coming clean to the people she loved. It wouldn't be easy, she realized. Matter of fact, other than saying goodbye to Bess, it might just be the hardest thing she'd ever faced in her life. But holding on to secrets wasn't healthy and she'd reached a place in her life where she valued the idea of having no skeletons in her closet.

This moment of reckoning had been five years in the making. *Be brave*, she urged herself. Then and only then would she be able to live the life she'd always imagined.

Chapter Thirteen

Due to the late hour, Maya ended up crashing at her parents' house rather than driving home on dark back roads while exhausted. There was something comforting about staying overnight in the house she'd grown up in. She always managed to sleep soundly in her old bed. In the morning, she woke up early and took the dogs for a short walk, then went back to make breakfast for her parents. Pancakes. Sausages, eggs and grits. Fruit salad.

Knowing she had a bomb to drop on them made Maya want to do something special for them. Sitting down for a meal together would be the perfect segue to her confession. She prayed they would find a way to understand what she'd done.

"What did we do to deserve such a lovely spread?" Gigi Roberts asked as she sat down at the kitchen table along with her husband. With her sepia-colored skin and brown eyes flecked with caramel, her mother was a striking woman.

"You just happen to be the best parents a girl could ever ask for," Maya said. "I've been so busy lately I haven't been able to spend much quality time with the two of you." She wasn't buttering them up. It was simply the truth. She had received their unwavering support throughout her life. Despite the devastating death of their oldest child, Gigi and Vance had always made things special for Maya, whether it was celebrating her birthday or making sure she had the perfect prom dress.

Losing a sibling was one of the most traumatic things a person could endure. From what she'd learned since Bess's death, a parent outliving a child was even worse. Her family had walked through grief together, and although it was an ongoing process, they'd nurtured and supported one another from day one. Their bond remained intact.

"Maya, this is wonderful," Vance said as he dug into his food. "If I haven't said it before, I'm very proud of all you've done with the clinic and your dog shelter. I've been able to enjoy my retirement knowing Best Friends was in good hands. You're getting rave reviews all over Owl Creek."

Maya reached over and patted her dad's hand. "You inspired me to become a veterinarian after watching your dedication and love for animals. It's all I ever wanted to do. And that's all because of you."

"Oh, we know," her mother said. "Even as a kid you were fixing broken-winged birds and putting them back in their nests."

"And you went around with a little black vet bag checking in on all the animals nearby," Vance added, chuckling. "It was super adorable."

"I'm not sure all of our neighbors agreed," Maya said, laughing along with her parents.

After they finished their breakfast and Maya cleared the table, she asked her parents to sit down in the living room to talk with her. Once they were all settled, Maya took a deep breath and dove right in.

"I have something important to tell you," Maya said. "It's something that I should have told you a long time ago."

Gigi raised a hand to her throat. "This sounds serious. What's wrong?"

"Whatever it is, we're here for you," Vance

said, encouraging her with his eyes to continue.

"I hid some information from you because I didn't want to hurt you," Maya said in a halting voice. "You suffered so much after Bess died. I just never wanted you to feel that type of pain again." She paused to gather her thoughts. Maya knew she needed to just say it, but she didn't want to shock them too badly with her confession. "Before I left for Seattle…to attend vet school, I was diagnosed with leukemia."

Her parents went still. Her words had stunned them into silence. Maya hated the hurt looks that came over their faces, but she still had to forge ahead. After all this time, they deserved the unvarnished truth from her lips.

"It's the reason I ended things with Ace. I didn't want to cause any of you pain. You'd already been through one tragedy and I had no way of knowing if I would survive." She let out a sob. "I thought it was best to handle it on my own, so I did."

"Did you go through treatment?" Vance asked, sounding horrified.

She rubbed at her eyes. "Yes. In Seattle. That's where I was diagnosed when I went for my vet school interview. Thankfully, I was one of the fortunate ones. After three cycles of chemo, I went into remission. I was monitored for the next two years, at which time the doctors declared me cancer-free."

"And Ace? You didn't tell him, either?" Gigi asked, sounding startled.

Maya shook her head. She felt deeply ashamed. Saying it all out loud brought home how wrong she'd been to navigate her health crisis on her own. It had been tantamount to a lie, although she'd never viewed it that way. She'd considered herself a buffer between the tragic news and her loved ones. "Florence was the only one who knew the truth, and I made her promise not to tell anyone."

Vance put his head in his hands. "I can't believe you went through this without your family present." His voice cracked. "It makes me so sad that you didn't have us to lean on. Sweetheart, your mother and I would have been by your side in a heartbeat."

"That's a parent's job, to weather the storms with our children," her mother added. Tears were flowing down her face and she didn't bother wiping them away. "You're our baby."

"I know," she said, wringing her hands. "It was terribly wrong of me. Please forgive me."

"Of course we forgive you, Maya. Do you forgive us?" her father asked. "If we ever made you believe we weren't strong enough to support you through something this monumental, we're terribly sorry."

"Oh, Daddy, that wasn't it. Not at all," Maya said. She reached over and threw herself against his chest, wrapping her arms around him. "This is all on me. I did this. I thought that I was protecting everybody, but it wasn't my place to do that. I shouldn't have carried it all on my shoulders."

"We love you, Maya," her mother said, placing her arms around her so they were in a group hug. "And we are eternally grateful that you're still here with us."

"I am, too," Maya said in a soft voice. "I'm blessed beyond measure."

After a lot of tears were shed and they'd talked it out, Maya felt so much better about her situation. Her parents had been loving and full of forgiveness. It made her so incredibly hopeful about having a heartfelt conversation with Ace. Although she'd been anticipating the worst, she now knew it was possible to achieve understanding and redemption.

She couldn't keep up this charade with Ace any longer. It was time to come clean about why she'd ended things with him. Maya was buckling under the weight of keeping the secret. It wasn't a small matter, either. Because of her deception, she'd ended their loving relationship and offered him next to nothing by way of explanation. She wished that she could go back and relive that moment. Instead of breaking up with him, Maya would have told him all about her leukemia diagnosis and leaned on his broad shoulders for support.

If only it was possible, she thought.

If they were going to have a shot at a future together, she needed to tell Ace the truth and hope that he forgave her. It was that simple, yet achingly complex.

Lord, give me the strength to speak from the heart and tell Ace everything I've been keeping from him. Let his heart be open so he can forgive me for my mistakes. They were forged out of love for him, but he might struggle to see it that way.

Honesty would serve as a bridge between her and Ace. It was a huge step in moving toward a future with the only man she had ever loved. As nervous as she was, Maya was beginning to see the light shimmering at the end of the tunnel. All she had to do was take a leap of faith and believe that there was hope for the two of them. And pray that Ace cared enough about her to forgive the huge mistake she'd made.

Never in a million years had Ace ever imagined he would be reigniting a romance with Maya. When she'd offered him the lead position at the dog rescue he'd been surprised. This potential reconciliation between them floored him. He kept expecting to wake up and realize that he'd been dreaming. In the last few weeks Ace had learned a lot about himself as a man. Pride had kept him from going after Maya all those years ago and demanding answers. He hadn't wanted her to see his raw, naked emotions. He wasn't that man anymore.

Now, he was willing to peel back the layers like an onion if it meant rebuilding what had been torn down.

Ace felt a lightness that he hadn't experienced in years. For so long he'd convinced himself that walking through life alone suited him. He had packed up his feelings for Maya in the same way he'd stored away her diamond engagement ring in an antique cedar chest. But now, all of those romantic feelings had come roaring back to life. Or maybe they'd always been there under the surface. All that mattered now was the future. Never again would he let anything separate him from the love of his life. He would walk through fire to be with her.

He'd stopped dreaming about a life with Maya a long time ago. But now, hope shone like a beacon in the distance. He was so grateful to God for giving him a second chance with the woman of his dreams. Life was showing him how important it was to hold on to the people who truly mattered and not to allow pride to get in the way. His mother's death had shown him that tomorrow wasn't promised. He couldn't take anything for granted. Not Maya. Or family and friends. And not his beloved pups. For the first time in a long time, having it all was just within reach.

Just this morning Maya had invited him over this afternoon for coffee and to talk. He didn't really have to guess what she wanted to discuss. They'd both made it clear to one another that their past needed to be dissected if they were going to be together. All Ace really wanted was a few answers. In his mind, he considered it as closing one door so another one could be flung wide open. It was what he wanted more than anything. The very idea of creating something new with Maya made his chest tighten with exhilaration.

Maya's house was situated near the Gray Owl woods, a few miles down the road from Otis's house. He'd always admired it, well before Maya had returned to town and purchased the charming lodge-style home. It was big, much too large for one person living alone. He wondered if she'd bought the house in the hopes of settling down in Owl Creek and building a family. The idea warmed his insides.

Don't go getting ahead of yourself, he reminded himself. *You still have many bridges to cross with Maya. You're not at the finish line just yet.*

He stepped onto her wraparound porch, admiring the ceramic sculptures gracing the area. A wind chime hung from a nearby holder, making soft, melodic sounds. A golden retriever came running from behind the house, followed by a barking cocker spaniel. He bent over and patted the friendly retriever as the smaller dog continued to bark at him. Maya opened the front door and called the mouthy dog inside. "Sorry about that, Ace. Betty is lacking in good manners. I'm happy to see that Veronica treated you well. They're both rescues that I adopted."

"Betty and Veronica, hmm?" he asked, chuckling. "You always were a fan of the Archie comics."

"I still am," she said, ushering him across the threshold.

Once he stepped inside Ace couldn't help himself from looking around at all of the rustic touches. A huge stone fireplace sat in the living room, surrounded by comfy-looking love seats and a big couch. Brightly colored artwork hung on the walls. From what he'd heard around town, Maya's mother had become a brilliant artist. He figured some of these paintings were her creations. Maya led him down the hall to a large kitchen with copper pots hanging by her stove. The aromatic scent of coffee filled the air. From what he'd seen, Maya had made a beautiful home for herself. Within minutes they were seated next to each other at the table and Maya was serving up hazelnut coffee along with a plate of oatmeal cookies and gingersnaps.

"I've got some great news," he told her with a grin. "Leo has decided to adopt Daisy and her pups."

Maya let out a little squeal. "All of them?"

When Ace nodded, she said, "He's way too generous. I hope he's not getting in over his head."

Maya had a good point. Daisy and her pups would be a handful. But he also knew that his best friend was a very pragmatic man. He didn't dive headfirst into things without thinking them through. "The ranch will be a nice wide-open space for the dogs to run around and play. He's certain his whole family will be helping out with the dogs."

"Florence's boys will love having puppies to play with out there," she said.

"Thanks for inviting me over," Ace said as he sipped the heady brew. Hazelnut coffee was his favorite, and it pleased him that she remembered. The scent of ginger wafted under his nose and he reached for one of the cookies. Maya had always been a master baker.

"It's my pleasure. What do you think of the place?" she asked.

Ace looked around. "It's terrific. I always thought this place was a beauty. Nice to see you making it your own."

"Being back in Owl Creek has been a real blessing," Maya said.

"It's just like you always imagined. Going

to vet school and coming home to run a practice. You're living proof that hard work pays off."

Maya fiddled with her coffee cup. Her mood seemed a little bit off, but perhaps he was misreading things. He shouldn't expect things to be effortless.

"Ace, we need to talk. It's important." The ambience in the room suddenly shifted. Maya sounded somber.

He immediately flashed back to the day she'd ended things with him, when she'd started off their conversation with those same exact words. The rawness in her voice and her troubled expression caused his heart to thunder inside his chest. But he needed to believe in her, in them and in their future. He wasn't going to give up on them like he'd done in the past.

"Okay," he said, trying to stay calm. "I think we're way overdue for a discussion."

"You're right. If we're going to move forward and try again, I have to be completely honest with you. I don't want any secrets standing between us."

Secrets? He had no idea what she was talking about. His heart began beating fast. Something didn't feel right. Suddenly it felt as if all the good energy in the room had evaporated. He took a deep breath and reminded himself to relax.

Ace wanted things to work out so badly with Maya. He needed to remember that they both wanted the same thing—to be together.

"Whatever it is, you know I've got you, Maya. You can tell me anything. Good, bad or in-between." Feeling she needed his reassurance, Ace moved his seat closer toward her, then dipped his head down and pressed a tender kiss on her lips.

"I did what I did to spare you pain. Please don't forget that," she blurted out, grabbing his hand. Maya was clinging to him as if she was afraid he was slipping away from her. Fear emanated from her eyes.

"I won't," he promised. As the seconds ticked by his stomach was churning more and more. He wished she would just spit it out. It was nerve-racking watching her fall apart.

She pulled her hand away and bowed her head. "I wasn't fair to you…to us. I didn't tell you the truth five years ago." Maya's eyes were filled with dread. She was speaking really fast, as if she now wanted to get the words out as quickly as possible.

A sick feeling swept through him. "Slow

down. What are you talking about? What didn't you tell me?" he asked.

"I didn't end things between us because I didn't love you, Ace." Tears slid down her cheeks. "I adored you. You were the man of my dreams in every way possible. I found out I had leukemia and I didn't want to put you through my illness, especially after all you went through when your mother was sick."

Shock roared through him. *Leukemia?* She couldn't be serious! He took a few moments to let her words wash over him. "Wait a minute. You had leukemia? That's not possible." He shook his head in disbelief.

Tears slid down her cheeks. "Yes, it is possible," she said with a nod. "Do you remember when I wasn't feeling well before we broke up? I had those episodes of nausea and dizziness. I went to see the doctor when I was in Seattle interviewing for vet school, and after taking some tests they diagnosed me with leukemia."

Ace sank back against his chair. If he'd been standing, he feared his legs might have given out. He ran a shaky hand over his face. "Why? How could you hide something like that from me?"

She stared back at him with tear-filled eyes.

"I was really scared that I wasn't going to make it. The only person I confided in was Florence. I didn't even tell my parents. They'd already been through such agony when Bess died in the accident." She let out a mournful sound. "It's an ache in their soul that will never heal. And I didn't want to burden them with worrying about losing another child. Just like I didn't want to force you to endure another cancer diagnosis in someone you loved."

"You had no right to make all the choices for everyone!" Ace ground out the words with barely contained fury. "We had a right to know! I would have stood beside you, no matter what happened."

"I know that now, but back then I was operating from a place of fear. I let it consume me and all I could think about was protecting the people I loved from being hurt. It wasn't something I took lightly, Ace. I was terrified."

"So are you cured now?" he asked, praying she'd gotten a clean bill of health.

"Yes, Ace," she said, bobbing her head. "I've been cancer-free for many years."

"Well then, why didn't you tell me once you got better?" His voice sounded calm and cold. It was the very opposite of how he felt.

"You went into remission. Why couldn't you tell me the truth then?"

"How could I?" she asked. Her voice rang out in the stillness of her kitchen. "I'd hurt you, Ace, even though my whole reason for not telling you was to spare you pain. By that time, you'd risen to the top of the dog-sledding world. You were single-mindedly focused on your career. I couldn't turn your life upside down again. It would have been selfish."

Ace's lip curled. "Selfish? Are you kidding me? What you did was selfish. You made all the decisions for me." He rose abruptly from his chair, causing it to scrape across her hardwood floor. "I was left reeling when you ended things. I blamed myself, thinking I wasn't good enough for you or that I'd done something to make you fall out of love with me." He felt sick to his stomach as the memories crashed over him. "I was in pain, Maya. Rock-bottom, soul-crushing agony. It felt like every ounce of happiness left my life when you walked away from me. I literally had to crawl my way up from the bottom just to be able to breathe normally again." Ace felt as if he was reliving the most agonizing moments of his life, and it was incredibly hurtful to dredge up the memories he'd tried so hard to bury.

Maya quietly got up from the table and approached him. "Forgive me, Ace. I may not deserve it, but I'm asking you anyway. Take a chance on me. On us." Her voice broke, and his stomach twisted seeing her in so much distress. Her eyes were full of regret and her own pain.

He backed away from her, not trusting himself to be so close to her. Ace didn't want to bend. He didn't want to forgive her. "How can I? We lost five years due to the fact that you buried the truth. You lied, Maya, about something monumental. That lie changed the course of our lives."

"I know," she said in a low voice, ducking her head. "But if we still love each other... if we want to be together, we can push past this. I know it won't be easy, but it might be the best thing we've ever done."

He was through with trying. All it ever did was lead to heartache. "All I ever wanted was to love you. I never needed to be a dogsled racer to be complete. I would've been content just to be your guy." Tears burned his eyes. Whatever he'd believed about their future was gone in a puff of smoke. Poof.

All this time he'd ached over the loss of her, constantly questioning what he had done to make her fall out of love with him. In reality, Ace hadn't done a single thing wrong! Maya's illness had been the reason behind their breakup. She'd walked away from him and their love story, leaving him all alone and nearly broken.

"I need to get out of here." Through a haze of red he made his way toward the door, ignoring Maya's pleas to stay and talk things out. In his mind, there was absolutely nothing left to discuss.

He'd rather be alone than wade his way through lies. That way he would never get hurt again. This was what happened when you let down your guard. He wouldn't ever again dare to dream that he was going to find everlasting happiness.

If this was love, Ace didn't want anything to do with it.

Chapter Fourteen

Maya didn't have the heart to look out the window and watch as Ace exited her life. She had no idea if they could continue to have a working relationship after this blowup, but it was clear Ace wanted nothing more to do with her romantically. And who could blame him? She'd broken all the trust between them. She'd always tried to tell herself her actions had been based on good intentions, but she hadn't been truthful. In the end, she'd done way more harm than good.

The heartache Maya was enduring right now was worse than the first time. It rivaled what she'd felt when Bess died. Having Ace ripped away from her for a second time was agonizing. She almost wanted to curl up into a little ball. She couldn't focus on anything

other than the devastated look on his face and
the things he'd said to her.

*What you did was selfish. You made all the
decisions for me.*

His words echoed in her mind, reminding
her of her foolish choices. Back then her decision had seemed as if it was the right one.
She'd spared all of her loved ones the pain of
having to deal with her illness. But now, after
seeing the situation through Ace's eyes, she
saw her actions in a different light. Control-
ling. Shortsighted. Unkind.

She pulled herself together to head to the
clinic for a few hours. Maya was interviewing Tiffany Battles, the potential new veterinarian for the practice, and giving her a tour
of the office. She also had a few patients to
check on. It took all her might to drive over
to the clinic without sobbing the entire way.
As it was, she felt certain her eyes were red-
rimmed and puffy. On her way into the office, she crossed paths with Zach, who was
working at the shelter today and training volunteers.

He greeted her with a smile. "Hey, Maya.
I didn't know you were coming in today."

"I just have a few things to do, then I can
go home. I want to check in on Daisy and her

puppies to make sure they're all doing okay. In a few weeks they can go home to the Duggan ranch," she explained. She did her best to keep her tone upbeat. Zach didn't need to get dragged into her and Ace's drama.

"Nice," he said with a nod. "The new volunteers are working out really well. They're a great addition to the shelter."

"Thanks, Zach. That's good to hear. You're doing a nice job. It hasn't gone unnoticed."

A blush spread across his face. "That's nice of you to say so. It's been great working with Ace." He wrinkled his nose. "We're much closer now. We grew apart when he was away from Owl Creek racing and training his sled dogs."

"It's a demanding profession. I'm really happy that the two of you have been able to bond." If she'd done nothing else, perhaps she'd played a role in bridging the gap between Ace and his little brother by bringing them both on board at the shelter. It raised her spirits a little bit. She hadn't just been a human wrecking ball in Ace's life.

"Can I just say that it's been great seeing Ace mellowing out a bit? That's all your doing. Ever since he started working at the dog rescue, he's changed. You've softened that chip on his shoulder."

Little did Zach know that Ace didn't want anything to do with her. The thought made her sick to her stomach. She couldn't smile and pretend as if things were great between her and Ace. She just couldn't do it.

"Are you okay, Maya? If I'm talking out of turn, I'm really sorry. It's just that I can see there's still a spark there... It's obvious every time you're in the same space."

"No. Don't worry," she said softly. "It's just... We've taken a few steps back in our relationship." She looked away from his intense gaze. "Things aren't great between us at the moment," she admitted. "It seemed as if we were in such a good place..." Her voice trailed off.

Zach let out a groan. "Maya, please don't give up on him. He's better with you in his life. My mother used to always say that and it's true."

His words felt like a punch to the gut. Suddenly she felt as if she'd let down Gloriana by not holding on to Ace hard enough and making such a mess of things.

"I haven't given up on him, Zach. He's stopped believing in me, and to tell you the truth, I don't blame him one bit." On the verge of tears, Maya knew she had to head inside before more waterworks commenced. "I'll see you later. I need to check on these pups."

Maya entered the clinic and greeted everyone she passed with a plastered-on smile. She needed to hold it together and just keep moving forward, the same way she'd done five years earlier. Heartbreak was nothing new to Maya. A part of her felt numb to it. She'd weathered it last time while undergoing grueling cancer treatment. If she could do that, this time around should be a breeze.

Even as the thought crossed her mind, Maya knew it wasn't true. The love she felt for Ace would endure for a lifetime. She would spend the rest of her days adoring a man who couldn't stand the sight of her.

Ace was still furious. He'd driven around Owl Creek for hours trying to soothe his anger and heartache. He and Maya had lost so much time when they could have been making a life together. Loving one another. Creating a family. And they would never get those moments back. He couldn't wrap his head around her deception. He ached inside.

What kind of person hid information like that from the man they'd claimed to love? he asked himself. They could have battled all of their storms together. She'd lost faith in him and in their love. There was no other way to look at it. Couples fought through the bad times together, leaning on each other for strength. That's what his parents had done when his mother fell ill.

He couldn't see his way past her huge lie.

When he reached his dad's house, Ace didn't even have the wherewithal to play with his dogs outside. He felt completely defeated. Luna trailed after him like a shadow, seeming to sense that he needed her company. Throughout his ride he'd kept asking God why. Why was he on this roller coaster with Maya? Why had the rug been pulled out from under him again?

As he entered the house through the back door, it slammed behind him.

Blue stood by the kitchen counter scowling at him. "What are you trying to do? Break it?" he asked.

"Of course not. That door always makes a racket," Ace barked.

Blue furrowed his brow. "What's wrong with you? You look lower than an ant's belly."

"Nothing," he muttered, placing his keys down on the table with a thud. He began to pace around the kitchen.

Blue eyed him warily. "Now if that isn't a straight-up falsehood, I don't know what is. Talk to me, son. Did something happen at the dog rescue?"

"No, everything is going well there," he answered.

His father scanned his face for a few seconds. "It's Maya. I can see it written all over you. Nothing else in this world could get you so fired up."

Ace let out a groan. "Like an idiot I fell in love with her all over again. Against all odds we found our way back to one another."

Blue grinned. "And? That sounds wonderful."

"Not exactly. I just found out that she's been lying to me ever since she broke up with me."

"That doesn't sound like Maya," Blue murmured, sinking down into a chair and placing his arms on the table.

He quickly gave Blue the rundown about Maya's confession.

"And all for what? She prevented all of her loved ones from knowing the truth about her being sick. I can't stop thinking, what if she hadn't made it? Didn't she think we deserved a heads-up?" All of his frustration was pouring out of him. They had been so close to a reconciliation. He couldn't wrap his head around Maya's actions. How was it possible that this was the same woman who'd always been honest to a fault?

Blue cleared his throat. "From what I'm hearing, it sounds like Maya felt as if she had to protect everyone."

"But that wasn't her role," Ace said. "I was her boyfriend, not some little kid she needed to shield." He leaned against the counter, feeling too antsy to take a seat.

Ace met his father's gaze from across the table. He could tell he was gearing about to get his point across. "Ace, try to think of it from her point of view. After Bess died, Maya's role in her family shifted. She went from being the baby of the family to the only child of parents who'd tragically lost one. From that point on it was her job to protect Vance and Gigi. You may not have picked up on it over the years, but I sure did."

Ace frowned. He hadn't noticed it all that much if he was being honest. But now that his father mentioned it, he realized it was true.

"But it still didn't give her the right to lie to everyone. That's not how you treat a partner."

Blue nodded. "I agree with you, but what I've learned in my life is that it's hard to judge people by their worst moments." He splayed his hands in front of him. "I wasn't planning to tell you about the looming foreclosure. I didn't want to hurt or disappoint you, son. If you hadn't been there when Dane came by it would have all blown up in my face."

"It seems we both have an abundance of pride," Ace said ruefully. "You could have told me. I would have understood."

The older man shrugged. "It was hard to know in that moment which path to take. I'm sure Maya felt the same way. And what she was dealing with was infinitely more stressful than my situation. It was a matter of life and death."

Maya's life had hung in the balance. His chest tightened as the grim reality took hold of him. She could have died of leukemia. And they would never have been able to reconnect, as they'd done over the past weeks. He would never have been able to kiss her. They never would have laughed together or talked about dogs or the shelter. And he never would have known that she hadn't fallen out of love with him when she'd ended things.

"Think of your mother, Ace, and how badly she suffered. And she wasn't alone on her journey. Not even for a single day. So imagine what Maya went through with nobody to lean on in Seattle." He let out a sigh. "That's a big burden on one person's shoulders."

"But she chose that path," he said, his heart cracking at the notion of Maya suffering so much when she'd been so far away from home.

"That's the thing about true love, Ace. It endures. At the end of the day, your mother and I always forgave each other's trespasses. Why, you might ask? Because we knew both of us were flawed and fully capable of making mistakes. The payoff of sticking it out and choosing love was monumental." Tears glistened in his eyes. "We both know life doesn't hand us many second chances."

Ace knew what his father said was true. He'd been thinking about it for weeks now. As he and Maya had grown closer with each day that passed, Ace felt grateful for being able to reconnect with her. When his grandmother had fallen, he'd watched his grandfather pray and hope and love as hard as he possibly could. He wanted that type of devotion. He wanted to be that type of man.

"I don't know what to do," he said as a hundred different thoughts tugged at him.

"Don't you, Ace? How many times does a person get a do-over? You still have a shot at having everything you've ever wanted." Blue wagged his finger at him. "Don't blow it."

Ace needed some fresh air. He needed to think it all through. Blue didn't say another word when Ace headed outside with Luna. His father knew him better than anyone, and he was aware of how he processed things. Being in the fresh Alaskan air with his dogs would give him the clarity he needed. When he entered the dog enclosure, all of his pups ran toward him at breakneck speed and quickly surrounded him. Ace got down on his haunches and allowed himself to be swarmed by the dogs, who were full of affection and spunk. This was his life. And he loved it. But there was a void in his world, and there had been for a very long time.

This was the very spot where he and Maya had talked about a future filled with their mutual love of dogs, their faith and family. *Beautiful, sweet Maya.* She'd weathered leukemia all by herself, with only Florence to confide in. She must have been terrified and lonely, and second-guessing her decision. He wished he'd been there for her to lean on, to confide in and to pray with. Ace could have been her anchor.

But you can still weather all the storms of life together. That's what his mother would have said to him. She would have reminded him that it wasn't too late to make things right with Maya. And she would have been right. Ace was tired of being without the woman he loved. She'd done the wrong thing, but she was human. She hadn't acted maliciously or with cruelty. She'd done something foolish out of concern for others.

He needed to offer her grace.

Even if he tried, Ace couldn't stop loving Maya. She was his other half. If he walked away from her, he would regret it for the rest of his days. He wouldn't be living out his best life without the woman he adored. He looked up at the beautiful Alaskan sky and the glorious sun trying to break through the clouds. If God was trying to tell him something, Ace was listening. There was no time like the present to claim his happily-ever-after.

By the time Maya returned home, it was almost dinnertime. She heated up some leftover eggplant parmigiana in the microwave and paired it with a small salad. Everything tasted like cardboard, so she ended up scraping her plate into the trash. Maybe cleaning out her closet would give her something to focus on. It would make her feel good to donate her gently used clothing items to a good cause. When she went in her bedroom, Maya turned on her iTunes and began to fish out garments from her closet as she danced around the room. Music had a way of lifting her mood and this time was no exception. It didn't take Maya long to fill up two garbage bags.

A sudden banging sound gave her a start. Maya turned down the music just as the sound repeated itself. The noise was so loud, she wondered if a bear had come calling again. It wasn't impossible. This time of year bears were coming out of hibernation and new cubs were exploring their territory. Last year a mama bear and her cubs had tried to come through her front door by charging their way in. It was one of those incidents that Maya knew she would never forget.

Maya peered out the window and spotted a truck in her driveway. It was too dark to see it clearly. Who would be paying her a visit at night? As she hurried downstairs, she wondered if it was someone seeking medical assistance for a wounded animal. Everyone in town knew where she lived. She jerked open the door, her entire body tightening up as she came face-to-face again with Ace.

Oh, no! She didn't think she could withstand another go-round if he'd decided to tell her all over again how awful she was. Not that he didn't have every right to be upset with her, but her heart couldn't bear any more pain. As it was, Maya just wanted to burrow herself away from the world while she healed. She hadn't fully opened the door. It felt like doing so would be an invitation for him to rake her over the coals again.

"Maya, I really need to talk to you." Unlike before, his voice sounded calm now. His expression was neutral, which was almost worse than before. She had no idea what he was feeling at the moment.

How could she deny him an audience after what she'd done? She really wasn't in any position to turn him down.

"All right," she said, shifting from one foot to the other. She just wanted to get this over with as soon as possible.

He reached out and gently pulled her by her

hands onto the porch. Maya didn't say a word or resist in any way. She was so shocked that he was touching her.

"Wh-what are you doing?" she finally asked as he released her hands. She wrapped her arms around her waist to ward off the chill. It was nippy outside.

"I love you, Maya. I always have." Ace smoothed his hand across her cheek. "And I don't see that ever changing."

Her knees went weak. Had Ace just declared his love for her? Surely she'd misheard him. How could this wonderful man love her after what she'd put him through?

"What did you say?" she asked in a raspy voice.

A hint of a smile played around his lips. "I said that I love you, Maya Anne Roberts. And if you'll let me, I want to shout it from the rooftops so everyone in Owl Creek knows."

She let out a stunned laugh. "Is that why you brought me outside?"

"No," he said. "I wanted to tell you how I feel right here in the Alaskan outdoors, where there's nothing but sky and stars and moon. For so long there's been so many things separating us. Being out here makes things really simple," Ace said, throwing his hands in the air and spreading them wide. "I love you, and I'm pretty sure you love me, too. That's the only thing that matters at the end of the day." Ace laced their hands together. "I'm so sorry that I let my pride take center stage earlier."

"You were so angry with me," Maya said, blinking away tears. "I never thought I'd hear those words ever again coming from your lips, but it sounds so beautiful." Maya let out a sob. She'd been waiting for this moment for five long years, never daring to dream it could really happen.

"Your life was saved. God held you in the palm of His hand and shepherded you through a terrible storm. How could I not be humbled and in awe of His greatness and your ability to push through such adversity? I'd be the world's biggest fool to walk away from you when all I've ever wanted is to be with you."

"Oh, Ace. That's all I want as well. And I love you, more than I did before if that's possible."

"Same here. I want our love to grow and expand, Maya," Ace said. "We can be so much stronger together than we could ever be apart."

Maya nodded. "I don't want to spend another moment without you."

"You won't have to. That's a promise," he murmured as Maya reached up and placed her arms around his neck, then pulled down his head for a romantic, soul-stirring kiss.

As the kiss ended, a shooting star flashed across the sky, cementing everything they felt about their happily-ever-after.

Epilogue

Maya looked out over the outdoor dog enclosure and sighed. This, she thought, was her own special brand of paradise. She released a carefree laugh as she watched Zach being chased by a tiny Chihuahua who was making loud yipping noises. He was so dedicated to the rescue dogs, much like his older brother. Together they had made the Owl Creek Dog Rescue a haven for dogs in need.

So many dogs had found their forever homes in the past few months. People had come from far and wide to adopt them. She thought South Korea may have been the farthest location, which boggled the mind. Ace's idea to promote the rescue dogs on a website and Instagram had been hugely successful. It allowed the public to connect with the dogs through pictures and videos even before meeting them in person.

For Maya, it was a long-held dream come true. These abandoned dogs were being bombarded with love and devotion. Of course, there were certain dogs still waiting to be adopted, but Maya felt confident that they, too, would find their forever families.

She sensed Ace before she felt him wrap his arms around her middle from behind her. "Miss me?" he whispered in her ear. She turned her head slightly to the side and met his lips as he leaned down and kissed her.

"Always," she said in a low voice, "but I'm grateful you're back."

Zach had been holding down the fort at the shelter while Ace traveled to Anchorage for an event with the foundation. He had provided an update about the dog rescue, detailing all the success they'd had with their adoptions and rehabilitations.

He turned her around so they were facing each other. "Guess what?" he asked, excitement radiating off him in waves.

"What? Don't tell me you came home with a few more rescues?" she asked, jokingly peering behind him as if she was looking for more dogs.

Ace threw back his head in laughter. "I know better than to do something like that without giving you a heads-up. We're already up to our ears in dogs." He paused dramatically. "They gave us more grant money."

Maya let out a cry of sheer joy and excitement. "They did? Oh, that's wonderful. I wasn't expecting anything like that."

Ace grinned. "Neither was I, babe. They heard everything I had to say about our shelter before announcing that they were happy to be giving us additional grant money so we can continue to make a difference."

"What an incredible blessing," Maya said, dabbing at her eyes. No matter how much she told herself not to cry and get emotional over things, she always ended up teary-eyed. At least these were tears born out of joy, she reminded herself. Life was good in so many ways. Her relationship with Ace had picked up right where they'd left off so many years ago. They were devoted to each other and, although neither had said it in words, Maya had the feeling they both intended to walk through life together.

"We have an abundance of blessings," Ace murmured, trailing his finger down the side of her face. He swung his gaze toward the enclosure and called out to Luna. Moments later, the dog was standing by Ace's side, looking up at him adoringly. "Hey, girl," he crooned, lovingly patting her on the head. "Thanks for helping me out."

Ace reached down and began fiddling with a ribbon tied around Luna's neck. Maya had no idea how it had gotten there unless Zach was playing a prank. Ace tugged at the ribbon and it broke free. A diamond ring hung from it. Suddenly, Ace got down on bended knee as Zach let out a loud holler of approval from twenty feet away. Maya let out a squeal, then covered her face with her hands. Although she'd been dreaming of this moment for a very long time, she hadn't been expecting it to happen right now.

"It's been a long time coming, but today's a very special day. I get to ask the most beautiful woman in the world if she'll marry me. We've spent way too many years apart. And all I want to do is spend forever with you. Will you marry me?" he asked, holding up the ring. "Will you say yes to nights gazing up at the moon and dropping everything to take care of a rescue dog? Will you dance in the snow with me and promise to kiss me every single day for the rest of our lives?"

By this time Maya was crying and laughing and trying to keep her composure so she could give Ace an answer. "Oh, I will. I do," she cried out. "I'll marry you. Anytime. Anywhere. Anyplace." Ace stood up and Maya flung herself at his chest, tightly wrapping her arms around his neck. When she finally let go, Ace took her hand and slid the ring on her finger, then placed a celebratory kiss on her lips. When the kiss ended, Maya spotted moisture lurking in the depths of his eyes. Even though Ace tried to be a tough guy, he was a teddy bear at his core.

"Did she say yes?" Zach called out.

"She did!" Ace said, holding up Maya's ring hand as proof.

"I did!" Maya shouted, letting out a squeal as Ace lifted her up by the waist and spun her around. She already felt dizzy with excitement, so being whirled around left her breathless.

Zach began clanging some pots together, creating a ruckus. Clearly, he'd been aware of Ace's plan and he'd been prepared to celebrate.

"Put me down, Ace," she instructed him, holding on to his arm to steady herself.

"I may just be the happiest man in the

whole world. I feel as if everything that was taken away from us has been restored."

"We have a fresh start, Ace. And anything is possible. If you want to get back into dog mushing, I'll support that one hundred percent."

He held her face between his hands. "And if you want to expand the clinic or the shelter, I'll be right by your side helping you out. We're in this together. For the rest of our days."

"We have so much to look forward to," Maya said, reaching up and lacing her hands around Ace's neck. When she looked up into his eyes she saw their amazing future reflected back at her.

"A life full of adventure," Ace said.

"And dogs," she said with a giggle. "Lots and lots of dogs."

"Let's seal that with a kiss," Ace suggested, wiggling his eyebrows.

"You don't have to tell me twice," Maya said, raising herself on her tippy toes and pressing a kiss on her future husband's lips.

They both knew forever was waiting for them.

* * * * *

*If you enjoyed this story,
look for these other Owl Creek books
by Belle Calhoune:*

Her Secret Alaskan Family
An Alaskan Twin Surprise
Alaskan Christmas Redemption
Hiding in Alaska

Dear Reader,

Thank you for reading Ace and Maya's story. Welcome back to Owl Creek! I had so much fun writing this reunion romance. There's nothing sweeter than two people reuniting after spending years apart. Maya Roberts is a kind and well-meaning heroine whose past actions torpedoed her relationship with the hero, Ace. Despite her best intentions, hiding the truth about her leukemia diagnosis was an act of betrayal in Ace's eyes. Ace Reynolds is a man who has lost a lot in his life. He's at a crossroads when he agrees to head the dog rescue. He's not a man who allows himself to be vulnerable, so it's a big deal for him to let Maya back into his life.

For me, this story raises the question of what is forgivable in a relationship. Can trust be rebuilt? Although this is romantic fiction, real people make choices like this each and every day. Maya's faith has seen her through her medical crisis and the death of her sister while Ace walks through the world as a man of faith. He's suffered a lot of losses over the years, but he steps out on faith to try again with Maya. Ultimately, this story is about forgiveness and holding on to love.

I love writing for Harlequin Love Inspired and this is my fifteenth book for the line.

Blessings,
Belle

Get 4 FREE REWARDS!
We'll send you 2 FREE Books plus 2 FREE Mystery Gifts.

FREE
Value Over
$20

Both the **Harlequin® Special Edition** and **Harlequin® Heartwarming™** series feature compelling novels filled with stories of love and strength where the bonds of friendship, family and community unite.

YES! Please send me 2 FREE novels from the Harlequin Special Edition or Harlequin Heartwarming series and my 2 FREE gifts (gifts are worth about $10 retail). After receiving them, if I don't wish to receive any more books, I can return the shipping statement marked "cancel." If I don't cancel, I will receive 6 brand-new Harlequin Special Edition books every month and be billed just $4.99 each in the U.S or $5.74 each in Canada, a savings of at least 17% off the cover price or 4 brand-new Harlequin Heartwarming Larger-Print books every month and be billed just $5.74 each in the U.S. or $6.24 each in Canada, a savings of at least 21% off the cover price. It's quite a bargain! Shipping and handling is just 50¢ per book in the U.S. and $1.25 per book in Canada.* I understand that accepting the 2 free books and gifts places me under no obligation to buy anything. I can always return a shipment and cancel at any time. The free books and gifts are mine to keep no matter what I decide.

Choose one: ☐ **Harlequin Special Edition**
(235/335 HDN GNMP)
☐ **Harlequin Heartwarming**
Larger-Print
(161/361 HDN GNPZ)

Name (please print)

Address   Apt. #

City   State/Province   Zip/Postal Code

Email: Please check this box ☐ if you would like to receive newsletters and promotional emails from Harlequin Enterprises ULC and its affiliates. You can unsubscribe anytime.

Mail to the Harlequin Reader Service:
IN U.S.A.: P.O. Box 1341, Buffalo, NY 14240-8531
IN CANADA: P.O. Box 603, Fort Erie, Ontario L2A 5X3

Want to try 2 free books from another series! Call 1-800-873-8635 or visit www.ReaderService.com.

HSEHW22

COUNTRY LEGACY COLLECTION

19 FREE BOOKS IN ALL!

EMMETT
Diana Palmer

COURTED BY THE COWBOY

THE RANCHER AND THE BABY
Marie Ferrarella

Cowboys, adventure and romance await you in this new collection! Enjoy superb reading all year long with books by bestselling authors like Diana Palmer, Sasha Summers and Marie Ferrarella!

YES! Please send me the **Country Legacy Collection!** This collection begins with 3 FREE books and 2 FREE gifts in the first shipment. Along with my 3 free books, I'll also get 3 more books from the **Country Legacy Collection**, which I may either return and owe nothing or keep for the low price of $24.60 U.S./$28.12 CDN each plus $2.99 U.S./$7.49 CDN for shipping and handling per shipment*. If I decide to continue, about once a month for 8 months, I will get 6 or 7 more books but will only pay for 4. That means 2 or 3 books in every shipment will be FREE! If I decide to keep the entire collection, I'll have paid for only 32 books because 19 are FREE! I understand that accepting the 3 free books and gifts places me under no obligation to buy anything. I can always return a shipment and cancel at any time. My free books and gifts are mine to keep no matter what I decide.

☐ 275 HCK 1939   ☐ 475 HCK 1939

Name (please print)

Address   Apt. #

City   State/Province   Zip/Postal Code

Mail to the Harlequin Reader Service:
IN U.S.A.: P.O. Box 1341, Buffalo, NY 14240-8571
IN CANADA: P.O. Box 603, Fort Erie, Ontario L2A 5X3